BLAME THE BLIZZARD

A SALTWATER SPRINGS HOLIDAY NOVELLA

TANISHA HEADLEY

ALSO BY TANISHA HEADLEY

THE SALTWATER SPRINGS SERIES

Beyond the Break

Below the Barrel

Blame the Blizzard

STANDALONES

Teach Me to Fly

For the love we lose, the love we chase, and the love that always finds its way home.

CONTENT WARNINGS

Some details of the professional snowboarding, skiing, and surfing world have been altered for your reading enjoyment.

To check content warnings for this book, visit tanishaheadley.com/content-warnings

PLAYLIST

Snow - Angus & Julia Stone
Cigarette Daydreams - Cage The Elephant
Ghost - Jacob Lee
TALK ME DOWN - Troye Sivan
Bad Dreams - Cannons
Cool Girl - Tove Lo
All I Want - Kodaline
Without You - Oh Wonder
Can't Pretend - Tom Odell
Forever - Lewis Capaldi
Electric Love - BORNS
Wild Love - James Bay
Mountain Sound - Of Monsters and Men

ONE

STERLING

SHE'S A DAMN BEAUTY.

I stare at the surfboard I just finished making with bated breath. The lighting in the shaping room is crap—one flickering overhead bulb and a shop window half-frosted from the cold—but she still shines. Pale teal resin over a soft swallowtail shape, triple stringer for stiffness, and just the right curve in the rocker.

I run a hand along the rail, relishing in the smoothness. She's sleek, and fast. I know she'll be a beast in the water, cutting through current like butter.

She deserves better than this room, I think to myself. Too bad the ocean's closed for business.

It's dead quiet, except for the faint tick of the heater and the occasional groan of the storm that's hammering Saltwater Springs. I glance out the little window and frown. Snow blows in sheets across the gravel lot, and the gray sky looks ready to stage the apocalypse.

There's no breeze off the ocean today, which means there's no swell and no surf. Just cold, wet silence.

That's the part that gets me. This board is ready, and there's no one even left to ride her. The Saltwater Shredders, the town's local surf team, packed up and flew to Hawaii two days ago to chase clean waves and sunshine, and I can't blame them. The storm hit hard and fast. Dumping two feet of snow in less than twenty-four hours and scaring off the last of the tourists. Now it's just me, the storm, and a dozen riderless boards stacked in the corner.

I head to the front of the shop where the cold half-drank coffee that I've already microwaved twice sits. I microwave it for a third time and lean against the counter, staring at the "CLOSED FOR STORM" sign I taped to the door.

The power flickers and the heater coughs.

I should be in Hawaii with the team, or anywhere warm for that matter, but I've never been one to follow the crowd. The moment something feels too easy or too settled, I pull the chute.

But this feels settled. And I hate it.

I pull out my phone and shoot off a text to my best friend.

STERLING:

> Are you still alive over in Bluewater Bluffs, or did that ski hill of yours get swallowed by snow?

Levi replies almost instantly.

LEVI:

> Alive and thriving. Powder's insane. You stuck in Saltwater Springs?

STERLING:

> Buried. Everyone bailed and the surf's dead. It's a ghost town.

LEVI:

Why don't you come work at my mountain resort for the rest of the season? You'd love it. My main instructor bailed for Banff.

STERLING:

Teaching snowboard lessons to bratty tourists?

LEVI:

Yeah, but hot tourists. In ski suits. With trust funds. Just saying.

I stare at the message, then look around the shop. At the stacked boards collecting dust, the snow hammering the windows, and the version of me I'm slowly becoming—settled.

Yeah. I need a reset.

STERLING:

Where would I stay?

LEVI:

Job comes with room at my family mountain chalet and a decent paycheck.

STERLING:

Damn. Hard offer to pass up.

LEVI:

I knew you'd cave. Pack your shit. I'll meet you at the bottom of Bluff Mountain.

"IT's BEEN WAY TOO long since I last saw you, man." Levi's voice cuts through the hum of the engine as we wind up the narrow, snow-dusted roads of Bluff Mountain. Pine trees crowd the edges of the road, heavy with white, the peaks looming like shadows against a gray sky. He shoots me a quick grin. "What's it been, like three years? Why the hell haven't you visited?"

I lean my head against the passenger seat, eyes tracing the lines of the road before I turn to look at him. "Time flies when you're having fun," I say, flashing him a sheepish grin.

He barks out a laugh, the sound bouncing off the enclosed space of the truck. "Fun, huh? Let me guess—does that fun involve a girl?"

I shrug, shifting back to stare at the road ahead. "I don't really do *permanent* anymore. If anything, the fun involves girls, plural. With a capital S."

Levi throws his head back and laughs, smacking my shoulder before shaking his head, grinning wide. "Such a ladies' man. Haven't changed a damn bit." He sobers, if only slightly, his voice softening. "But seriously—I'm glad you're back. Even if it's just for a month."

"Yeah." I grunt, the sound more appreciative than it probably seems.

We round the last bend, tires crunching over the icy driveway, and his family chalet comes into view. I let out a low whistle. The place rises like a mountain itself, all stone and glass, with floor-to-ceiling windows reflecting the twilight. In the three years I've been away, I'd nearly forgotten just how loaded the Harts are, but being here now makes it impossible to ignore. This isn't a chalet; it's a damn castle.

"The infamous Hart Chalet," I mutter, eyes drinking in the sprawling deck and the peaked roofs. "Tell me you're staying here with me?"

Levi kills the engine and hops out without answering,

which is my first red flag. I climb out too, rounding the truck to meet him at the back. He fiddles with the latch, too focused on avoiding my eyes.

I let out a heavy sigh as I grab my duffel and snowboard once he gets the door open. "Spit it out, Levi. What's going on?"

"I'm not staying here with you," he says, finally meeting my gaze.

"Oh?" My brow quirks up, suspicion prickling. "So I'm staying here alone?"

He cringes, rubbing the back of his neck. "Not exactly."

My frown deepens. "What do you me—"

"Levi Carter Hart!"

The voice slices through the quiet mountain air, feminine, and far too familiar. I freeze while every muscle in my body locks tight as if the sound alone has claws.

Levi's guilty look is confirmation enough, but I barely register it because my heart is already climbing into my throat, pounding so hard I can feel it in my teeth.

Slowly and reluctantly, I turn toward the voice and there she is.

Maisy Hart.

Levi's little sister, and my ex-girlfriend.

The real reason I haven't set foot in Bluewater Bluffs in three years.

TWO

MAISY

LEAVE it to my dipshit older brother to blow up my winter plans by pawning off his best friend—who also happens to be my ex—at the family chalet that I specifically told him I was planning to stay at by myself.

Sterling's eyes find mine, and the breath catches in my throat, as a chill shudders through me. Three years. It's been three years since I last saw him, and somehow, he looks even better than the memory I've been trying to forget.

His skin is darker now, more bronzed than it usually is, from his endless days in that beach town he ran off to. His curls, once as dark as night, are streaked with sun-bleached strands. And those dark brown, all-consuming eyes I swore I'd never fall into again stare back at me.

There's no way in hell he can stay here.

With me.

Alone.

"Oh, come on, Maisy." Levi throws me a look, irritation peaking through his easygoing tone. "I don't have a spare room at the ski resort for him."

Sterling turns, brows drawing together. "What about the instructor that bailed for Banff? Can't I just stay in his room?"

Levi shakes his head, exasperated. "Cody lives in Bluewater Bluffs. He never stayed at the resort because he would always just drive up on workdays."

"Unbelievable." My arms cross tightly over my chest, hiding the angry tremor in my hands. "Levi, I told you I was coming up here for a month—for me. To focus and finally learn how to snowboard without a hundred eyes on me. How the hell am I supposed to do that with someone else in my space?"

"Maisy, stop being such a princess," Levi shoots back. "You'll still have your 'you time' while Sterling's at work. And as for your lessons..." He slaps a hand on Sterling's shoulder with a grin. "You couldn't ask for a better teacher."

"What?!" Sterling and I say in unison, our heads whipping toward him.

"I don't want any of the other instructors trying to get in your pants, Maisy. Sterling is the only person I trust to respect that boundary, given your past and all."

"I don't think this is a good idea, *given* our past," Sterling says.

"Exactly!" I shout. "What if we kill each other out there?"

Levi sighs, already checking his watch. "Come on, guys. Put your big-girl and big-boy pants on, bury the past, and deal with this. It's one month. Plus, who knows? It might even be fun."

I gape at him. Fun? My pulse is pounding, and Sterling looks like he's about to strangle him.

"I've got a group orientation in twenty minutes," Levi mutters, already backing away toward the truck. "You two will be fine. I promise."

He scrambles inside before Sterling can respond. Tires rolling over thin ice, and then he's gone, disappearing down the winding road and leaving me stranded in the silence of the chalet driveway with the one person I thought I'd never face again.

When Sterling finally turns his gaze back to me, it's like standing under a spotlight and feeling exposed. A million unsaid words ricochet through my head, none of them making it to my tongue.

"Are you coming in," I ask stiffly, "or are you planning to sulk out here all day?"

"I can call a taxi," he says flatly, pulling his phone from his pocket. "Find a hotel in town if that's easier."

And God help me, because a part of me wants to tell him to do it. To tell him to get the hell out of here. But another part of me—traitorous and buried deep—aches with something dangerously close to longing. For him. For us. For what we had before everything went to shit.

"Levi's right," I hear myself say, cutting him off before he can scroll. "We can be adults about this. We can share a roof without it being weird."

His mouth curves into a slow smirk, and my heart kicks so violently it feels like I've swallowed a grenade.

"Maisy Hart," he drawls, eyes glittering, "playing grown-up?"

I roll my eyes, heat crawling up my neck. "Whatever the hell that's supposed to mean." Spinning on my heel, I stalk toward the chalet, ignoring the wild thud of my pulse while knowing full well that his gaze is glued to my ass right now.

"I DON'T WANT you bringing back any snowbunnies into this place." My tone is firmer than I intended, and my grip tightens around my water bottle as I watch Sterling toe off his boots by the door.

He glances up, amusement tugging at his mouth. "Snow-bunnies? I thought you liked those fluffy little hoppers."

I roll my eyes, arms crossing tight over my chest. "You know exactly what I mean."

A low chuckle rumbles out of him as he looks away briefly, then back at me. His gaze catches and holds onto mine. "Relax, Hart. I wouldn't bring a girl here. I'm not a dick."

I arch a brow, disbelieving. "Really? Because rumor has it you've built quite the reputation with women these days."

His eyes spark with mischief, and he doesn't even bother to deny it. He just stares, silently, until the weight of what I said prickles under my skin. He tilts his head, lips curving. "Keeping tabs on me, Hart?"

Heat shoots up my neck, and I almost launch my water bottle at his infuriatingly smug, sexy face. "No, dick," I bite out. "All the girls you screw from this town make sure to gloat about it for weeks."

He hums, leaning his snowboard against the wall, voice dropping to almost teasing. "Hmm, it sounds like that bothers you."

"That has to be the stupidest thing you've ever said." My voice is flat, but my heart is racing. "I guess it wouldn't bother you if random guys from your little surf town came back brag-ging—in *graphic* detail—about how good they fucked me? Multiple times in one night?"

The change in his expression is immediate. His jaw tight-ens, shoulders coil, and something dark flashes in his eyes. He looks dangerous and...possessive? The sight sends a confusing rush through me—half satisfaction, half alarm. Because he looks like he'd kill the first guy who dared to put his hands on me. Why the hell does he still react like this after all these years?

"Point made," he mutters, low and clipped, breaking the tension by gazing around the chalet. "Which room is mine?"

I shrug, forcing nonchalance even though my chest still feels tight. "Whichever one you want. Just stay out of mine."

Without another word, he hoists his bag and walks down the hall, disappearing to claim his space. Leaving me standing with a water bottle in hand, trying to steady the riot in my chest.

THREE

STERLING

THE CHALET MIGHT LOOK like a damn mini-castle from the outside, but being stuck here with Maisy makes it feel more like I'm trapped in an elevator with nowhere to run. And for some fucking reason, this palace only has one bathroom.

We're standing across from each other, both of us gripping towels, the bathroom door between us.

"There's a million bedrooms in this place," I say, baffled, "but only one bathroom? Explain that math to me."

"A design flaw," she mutters, eyes narrowed. "But you're more than welcome to shower at the resort if it's a problem." Her hand lands on her hip, that little tilt of attitude making her glare more menacing.

"You want me to take a cab up the mountain just to take a shower?" I ask, incredulous.

She shrugs, already reaching for the knob. "By all means. Stay there, too. I hear the café benches are very supportive. Might be cozy enough for you to survive a whole month."

"So much for being an adult about this living situation," I mutter.

She tries to swing the door shut in my face, but I slip past her shoulder and push my way inside before she can.

Her head snaps toward me, glare dialed up to lethal. "Out." She points toward the door behind me like she's commanding a dog.

I grin and peel my hoodie over my head, my T-shirt riding up with it before settling back down. "Nah, I think I'll stay."

When I look at her again, her lips are parted, her glare faltering for a split second too long, and I catch exactly where her eyes are focused.

My smirk widens. "Careful, Hart. You're drooling."

Her nose wrinkles as she shoots me a glare, wiping at the corners of her mouth. "Please. You wish."

"Mhm." I chuckle, tossing my hoodie onto the counter. "If you say so."

Her cheeks flush as she brushes past me, deliberately bumping my shoulder on her way out, and I let out a quiet laugh once the door slams behind her.

She's still sexy as hell when she's mad.

I start the shower, the water hissing to life, and steam fills the room within minutes. I quickly undress and hop under the scalding water, letting it beat down on my back while I bask in the heat. After such a long time in a surf-town that rarely gets snow, my body forgot how to handle the extreme cold of a mountain.

I grab the bodywash that sits on the tiled floor, spray some out, and begin lathering it into my skin to wash away the day. It doesn't take long for my thoughts to find their way back to Maisy.

Surprise, surprise.

It's been three years since we ended things and yet here she is, still affecting me the same, as if nothing's changed.

I drag a hand through my wet curls, cursing under my

breath. Living here with her? For a month? Alone? No Levi running interference? It's a disaster waiting to happen.

She's off-limits ever since that night everything blew up between us. The night she admitted she blames me for her accident. And if the wreckage of that ending wasn't enough reason to keep my distance, there's the fact that Levi would snap my board in half, and then my neck right after if he even suspected I was looking at his little sister the wrong way.

Hell, he'd kill me twice if he thought I was touching her again.

I shut my eyes, letting the water pound over my face as I turn around, and force the thought out. Maisy Hart is history. She's a complication I don't need, in a place I came to have fun for the season. Whatever spark still flickers between us doesn't matter. Not anymore.

Once I've rinsed my body and my hair clean, I shut off the water and towel dry myself while repeating a mantra to myself.

Maisy is off-limits.

Maisy is Untouchable.

Maisy is Dangerous.

But deep down, I already know I'm lying to myself. Because in reality, I came here with the hopes of seeing her again, even if it was just from a distance.

"You're an asshole, you know that?" Maisy growls from behind me just as I turn off the stove.

"I've been told," I mutter, glancing at her over my shoulder.

Her dark hair looks even darker when wet, making her milky complexion and bright blue eyes stand out. She's still the most beautiful girl I've ever seen. I catch myself staring too long and force my gaze back to the pot, focusing on plating the pasta I made.

"You used all the hot water," she continues, stepping closer. "Do you know how cold the cold water is on a mountain?"

"You're telling me a place this size doesn't have an endless tank of hot water?" I finish plating and turn just as she reaches my side. "Here."

She blinks at the plate I hold out, her irritation softening into surprise. "What is that?"

"Dinner, Einstein."

"You can cook cook now?" She blinks. "I mean, you cooked for me?"

"I cooked for *us*," I correct, sliding the plate into her hand before turning back to make my own.

Maisy lingers for a moment, speechless, before quietly heading for the island. I grab my plate and drop onto the stool beside her. She's already twirling the pasta with her fork, chewing slowly, like she's suspicious I might've poisoned it.

"Well?" I ask, stabbing into my own pile.

Her brows jump up. "Not bad."

"Not bad? That's the highest compliment I think I've ever gotten out of you."

She smirks faintly but doesn't retort, choosing to go back to eating. I guess she really does like the food. The knowledge of that warms my chest, but I do my best to ignore it. For a moment, there's only the sound of forks scraping against the ceramic plates while the wind rattles outside the chalet.

"So," I start, leaning an elbow on the counter, "why do you want to learn snowboarding all of a sudden?"

She blinks at me. "What do you mean?"

"You're a two-time Olympic skier, Maisy." I gesture at her with my fork. "People pay money to watch you glide down mountains like you've got invisible wings. Why torture yourself learning something you'll just...suck at for a while?"

Her smile fades as she sets her fork down carefully, eyes fixed on the steam rising from her plate. "Because skiing doesn't feel the same anymore. I can't compete at the same level that I used to."

Her admission tightens my chest. It's not like her to get real this quick, she's always been the type that makes it feel like pulling teeth, but I keep my voice even. "Because of the accident."

Her blue eyes slide to mine. "Yes, because of the accident." She looks down again. "That day changed everything. My body, my confidence...me. I can't go back to who I was, no matter how much everyone wishes I could. And I'm tired of trying. So I decided that maybe it's time to figure out who I am now."

I swallow, my throat suddenly dry.

"And snowboarding is supposed to help with that?"

Her lips twitch, almost a smile but not quite. "It's different enough to challenge me. But it's still on the snow, still a mountain. It feels...familiar. Just not the same."

I study her profile, the curve of her jaw, the stubborn set of her mouth. There's something different about her that wasn't there three years ago. It makes me want to reach for her, to say something—anything—that might ease the heaviness between us, but I grip my fork tighter instead.

Because no matter how much she's changed, she's still Maisy.

And Maisy will always be off-limits.

FOUR

MAISY

"I KNOW it's been several years since I was a beginner at something, but I'm almost certain we should be on a bunny hill right now and not halfway up the fucking mountain, Sterling," I shout over the whistle of the wind.

It's my first day of snowboarding lessons and Sterling decided we'd start where the pros go. But I'm no pro.

Not at snowboarding at least.

"You're too good for a bunny hill, Hart. You just need a crash course in technique, and you'll be taking off down the slope just like everyone else."

"You sound like you have a lot of confidence in me," I say, looking at him now, but I can't see his eyes hidden under his goggles.

"'A lot' is a bit of a reach," he mutters, but I catch it.

Dick.

"Alright." Sterling claps his hands together, but his thick gloves mute the sound. "Let's start with figuring out which one of your feet is your front foot."

I blink at him. "Don't you already know that? You've seen me ski a thousand times."

"Yeah, but snowboarding's different." He steps closer, boots slightly sinking into the packed snow. "So we're gonna test it."

I narrow my eyes. "Test it how?"

Sterling plants his big, gloved hands on my shoulders and gives me a sudden shove.

"Sterling!" I squeal, stumbling forward in the snow. My right foot shoots out instinctively to catch myself.

"Ah-ha." He points, smug as hell. "Right foot goes forward. That's your stance."

I turn and glare at him. "You can't just shove someone down a mountain to figure that out!"

He chuckles, the sound low and infuriating. "But it worked, didn't it?"

"I should report you to my brother."

"You do that, sweetheart. After this lesson." He shoves his goggles up onto his helmet and kneels in front of my board, brushing snow off the bindings. "Okay, let's get you strapped in."

I awkwardly balance on one foot as he secures the first strap, his fingers moving with ease despite his thick gloves. He tugs on the second one, then frowns.

"What?" I ask, suddenly nervous.

He tugs again, harder this time, then sits back on his heels. "These bindings aren't right."

"Not right how?"

"They're too loose. You'll have no control over the board if your foot's sliding around. Who set you up with this rental?"

"Jeff, from the rental shop."

Sterling mutters something under his breath I can't quite catch, but it definitely isn't flattering. Then he looks up at me, eyes shadowed by his goggles. "If you'd tried riding like this, you could've wrecked your ankle. Or worse."

A chill runs through me, one that has nothing to do with the cool mountain air. The memory of the crash three years ago flashes through my mind—the snap of my ski, the blinding pain shooting up my spine before everything went numb, the way the world blurred as I lay there knowing in my gut something had broken that couldn't easily be fixed. I barely clawed my way back from that, and the doctors weren't subtle when they told me another serious injury could mean goodbye, not just to snow sports, but walking altogether.

That thought alone makes my stomach turn. I bite the inside of my cheek, trying to push the fear down before it swallows me whole. Sliding down mountains has been my entire life. Without it...who even am I?

"Don't look so scared," he says, softer now. "We'll fix it. But from now on, you don't ride during my lessons unless I've checked your gear first. Got it?"

I bristle at his bossy tone, but the way his voice dips lower makes my stomach flip.

"Got it," I mutter, even though I want to argue.

Sterling nods once, decisive, and starts working the straps tighter. His gloves brush my boots, and for one reckless second, I wish it were his hands on my bare skin instead.

He tightens the last strap with a grunt, then looks up at me from where he's crouched in the snow and the sight hits me like a sucker punch. Him, on his knees in front of me. Goggles pushed up on his forehead, brown eyes on me.

For a split second, it's three years ago, his hands on my thighs instead of my boots, his mouth against me, his gaze pinning me in place as if I were the only thing in his entire world. Him worshipping me until I came completely undone.

Heat rushes through me so fast it's dizzying and I blink hard, snapping myself back into the present.

"Alright," Sterling says, straightening, oblivious to the storm he just triggered inside of me. "That should hold. Try shifting your weight, see if it feels snug now."

I shift my weight, rocking heel to toe, testing the snugness. "It feels secure now."

"See?" Sterling says, stepping back, brushing snow from his gloves. "Now you won't go flying out of your bindings the second you point your board downhill. That's always a good start."

"Comforting," I deadpan, earning myself the faintest smirk from him.

He plants his board flat in the snow and motions toward me. "Alright, for your first lesson, you'll learn proper technique and probably figure out how to stand back up after a fall without looking like a turtle on its back."

"Great. Can't wait to be a professional turtle," I mutter, struggling to shift myself upright. My legs wobble, the board fighting me, and I almost pitch backward.

Sterling steps in immediately, steadying me with a gloved hand on my arm. "Relax. You're fighting it. Let the board do what it's built to do."

"Oh, so I'm supposed to trust the giant slippery piece of wood strapped to both my feet?"

"That's kind of the point, Hart." He crouches slightly, showing me how to angle my knees. "It's not that different from your skis—you trusted those to carry you, right? Same idea. Center of gravity low, chest over your knees. Like this. You'll feel more balanced."

Trusted my skis. I don't trust them anymore. Not since that day. Not since everything went wrong.

I mimic his stance, shaky at first, but when I settle into it something clicks and the wobbling eases.

"There you go," he says, his voice low and approving. "Now try a little slide."

"A what?"

He grins. "Just lift your front foot and let the board glide a few inches."

I do it, sliding maybe two feet before the board jerks awkwardly and I squeal, arms flailing. Sterling's laugh echoes across the snow as he grabs my elbow to steady me again.

"Not bad," he says, his eyes crinkling. "Better than I expected, honestly."

"Wow. I love how much faith you have in me," I shoot back, but I can't stop the small smile tugging at my lips.

"Don't worry," he says, dropping his voice, almost too soft for the wind to carry. "I've got you."

Sterling pulls his goggles back over his eyes and steps behind me, close enough that I can feel the heat radiating off him even through all the layers.

"Okay," he says, low and steady, "your shoulders are stiff. You've got to let them turn with your hips." His hands come down on my waist, firmly, guiding me through the motion.

The contact nearly short-circuits my brain. His palms are exactly where they used to be—where I used to *want* them—and it's all I can think about.

"Like this," he murmurs, twisting me gently.

I swallow hard, trying to pay attention, but my knees feel weak, my heart pounding like I'm back in one of those moments where his touch meant everything. The distraction is enough that when I try to shift my weight, my balance tips.

"Shit—"

I start to go down, but Sterling reacts instantly, wrapping his arms around me in an attempt to keep me upright. It doesn't work, and we tumble into the snow, with him taking most of the fall.

When the world stops spinning, I realize he's braced over me, one arm sunk into the snow beside my head. His chest presses into mine, his face only inches away, and my breath catches.

And then—God help me—I realize his thigh is wedged firmly between my legs, pressing exactly where I don't want to remember how good he used to make me feel.

The silence stretches, thick and charged. I can feel his breath fogging against my cheek. I may not be able to see his eyes through the goggles, but I know his gaze is locked on mine.

No. Absolutely not.

I shove at his chest, hard enough to topple him sideways into the snow.

"Smooth," I snap, sitting up and brushing snow from my jacket before shoving my goggles up. "Real professional. I bet all your students get this level of hands-on service?"

He smirks, propping himself up on an elbow and pushing his goggles up too. "Only the difficult ones."

"Difficult?" My eyes narrow.

"Yeah." His grin widens. "The ones who fight me every step of the way, but secretly love it."

I let out a fake laugh, reaching down to unclip from the board before pushing myself to my feet and brushing snow off my pants. "If you're waiting for me to start loving it, you'll be waiting longer than three years."

"Oh, yeah? How long, Hart?"

"A lifetime," I growl. "Eternity."

I grab the board, deliberately turning my back on him before he can fire back, but even with my back to him, I can feel his eyes on me. Heated and dangerous.

FIVE

STERLING

LATE AFTERNOON SUNLIGHT spills across the slopes, painting the snow gold and pink as the sun begins its slow decline behind the mountain.

It's quieter now that the big crowds have thinned out. Perfect conditions to glide down the mountain a couple times. Too bad I can't enjoy any of it—not with Maisy strapped to her snowboard in front of me, swaying like she's about to eat snow at any second.

"Alright," I call, closing the small gap between us. "Keep your shoulders angled downhill, and your knees soft. Stop fighting the board."

"I am soft," she snaps back, her nose scrunching under her goggles.

I bite back a laugh. "No, you're not. You're stiff as a board."

"I'm not stiff!" She bends her knees dramatically, overcompensating, and instantly wobbles back and forth.

I dart forward, my hands grabbing her elbows to steady her. Warmth floods through my gloves and I force myself to let go, stepping back like she burned me. Too close.

"Ready to start listening?" I ask, clearing my throat.

She glares. "You're a terrible teacher."

"No, you're just a terrible student." I grin, because pushing her buttons is too easy.

Her lips twitch like she's fighting a smile, and it nearly knocks the air out of me.

"Okay," I say quickly, needing to redirect before my brain goes somewhere it shouldn't. "We're gonna practice heel edge first. Lean back slightly, bend your knees almost like you're going to sit in a chair, dig your heels in, and let the board cut across the slope. Got it?"

Maisy nods like she's about to conquer the mountain. She pushes off, sliding downhill, and for a few blissful seconds, she's balanced—graceful even. But then, just as quickly, her weight shifts and she tips backwards.

"Sterling!" she yelps right before she goes down hard, snow exploding around her.

I'm laughing before I can stop myself and she rips off a glove, chucking it at me. I catch it easily, still laughing.

"Help me up, asshole!" she growls, sprawled on her back like a starfish.

I crouch down, grinning as I pull off my glove and offer her my hand. The second her fingers slip into mine, it's like a live wire is running through me.

It's too easy to remember how perfectly we used to fit.

Too easy to want it again.

As if I ever really stopped.

I yank her up fast, like ripping off a Band-Aid, then immediately step back, tossing her glove at her before sliding mine back on. "Try again."

Her cheeks are pink, but she doesn't fight me on it as she checks her straps. That's Maisy in a nutshell—too damn stubborn to quit.

The next run, she lasts longer. The one after that, she makes it ten whole feet without falling. Every time, I'm ready to catch her, fighting myself not to hold on longer than necessary.

By the time she finally makes it down to the second flag along the mountain, she's panting and her arms are shaking. But her smile—God, that smile—is so bright it twists my chest in knots.

"See?" she says, proudly. "Not a terrible student after all."

I shake my head, holding back the grin that's fighting to spread across my face. "You're still terrible. Just...less terrible."

She shoves me with her gloved hand, and it's stupid how badly I want to grab it and not let go. But no matter how good it feels to have her back in my arms, even for a second, Maisy Hart is off-limits.

She's beaming like she just won a gold medal, cheeks flushed as she stares up at me, and for a second, I forget where we are. I forget everything except how badly I want to pull her in and kiss her—

"Yo!"

I jolt, whipping my head up. Levi is walking toward us behind Maisy, snowboard tucked under his arm, instructor vest bright against the snow. His brows lift when he takes in the scene—Maisy sweaty and grinning, me standing way too close.

He smirks. "Well, look at that. My little sister's still alive. Didn't break your neck yet?"

"Not for lack of Sterling trying," Maisy mutters, shooting me a side-eye.

I bark out a laugh, mostly to cover the way guilt shoots through me as I stare back at my best friend.

"Alright, you comedians," Levi says, shaking his head. "Wrap it up. There's a wind warning rolling in, so we're shutting down the slopes early today. Last lift in twenty."

Maisy frowns. "Already? It's barely six."

"Yeah, well, blame Mother Nature." Levi shrugs, then points his gloved finger at me. "Don't keep her out too long. If she ends up frostbitten, it's on you."

"Relax, Dad," Maisy fires back. "I'll be fine."

Levi snorts, eyes jumping between us before his eyes find mine. My shoulders tense under the weight of our eye contact, and I see the silent warning in his stare.

Maisy is off-limits.

Levi jerks his chin at the base lodge. "Lights start going out in fifteen. Don't miss the lift unless you plan to attempt riding down the whole mountain, sis. I'll see you both at the bottom."

He chucks his board down and clips his boots in, sliding away and leaving behind a silence that's thick enough for me to choke on.

Maisy shakes her head. "He's worse than my parents sometimes."

"I'm sure he is," I mutter distractedly as I watch him go, though my chest remains tight.

She pushes off again, determined to squeeze in one last run, and I follow close behind her. The slope is even quieter now as skiers trickle down the mountain one by one. Each time she stumbles, I catch her. And each time, I have to remind myself to let go.

By the time we reach the third flag the floodlights are shutting off one by one, shadows swallowing the slope. The air has that eerie stillness before a storm.

Maisy stares down at the darkening slope, breath clouding in front of her. "Guess that's our cue."

"Yeah." I reach out automatically, brushing my gloved fingers against her arm to guide her back up the mountain. We're closer to the ski lift that brought us up the mountain than we are to the bottom.

The last row of lights blink out seconds later, plunging the hill into blue twilight. I jerk my chin toward the lift. "Come on. Let's catch the last ride down before we're stranded."

Her eyes meet mine, something like fear in them. Then she nods, and we head for the ski lift together.

SIX

MAISY

THE SKI LIFT creaks beneath us while it carries me and Sterling down the mountain, the cold air nipping at my cheeks. I hug the safety bar a little tighter than I want Sterling to notice, because I hate being this high. There's just too much empty air between me and the ground for it to feel safe. It never bothered me during my skiing career, but after the accident, being this high up is anxiety inducing.

"So, Saltwater Springs. That's where you ran off to, right?" I blurt out in an attempt to distract myself.

Sterling tips his head, one eyebrow raised. "Ran off? That's a dramatic way to put it."

"Well, you did vanish. One day you were here, the next you're suddenly this mysterious surf-town guy. What's it like there?"

He leans back, playing it cool, eyes shifting back to the dark trees below. "It's sunny and laid-back, and there are waves instead of snow. So a very different vibe from here."

"Mm." I study him from the corner of my eye. "And that's

27

what you wanted? Something different than what you had here?"

He nods and a sudden ache hits my chest at his admission. But I still want to know more.

"And what do you even do there all day? Just hang out on the beach and catch waves?"

"Sometimes." A little smirk tugs at his mouth. "Other times I shape boards for their local surf team."

"I bet you get plenty of girls," I say, instantly regretting how bothered I sound.

That earns me a sidelong, amused glance. "Why, jealous?"

Heat prickles at my neck, but I scoff. "Please. I just mean that it's a surf town. I can picture it now. Half-naked, tanned tourists everywhere. You probably don't even have to try and get girls, they just come flocking to you."

Sterling chuckles under his breath, low and maddening. "It's not as glamorous as you're imagining, Maisy."

I hug the bar tighter, rolling my eyes. "Right. I'm sure it's a real struggle. Poor Sterling, forced to live in a sunny paradise with an endless amount of girls and amazing weather."

His smile fades, voice dipping cooler. "You make it sound like I left just to chase a vacation."

"Didn't you?" The words come out harsher than I mean them to, and I know I'm being unreasonable, but I can't help myself. "You didn't exactly fight to stay."

His jaw tightens, eyes cutting to me. "Funny. I remember you being the one who walked away first."

Silence slams down between us and my stomach begins to knot, part regret, part stubborn pride. I grip the bar tighter, refusing to meet his eyes because we both know he's not wrong. I was the one that ended things between us. I was the one that walked away. But I'd be lying if I said a part of me hadn't wished he would chase after me back then, and fight harder to keep what we had.

Suddenly, the chair jolts and everything goes still, my stomach dropping to my ass. "No, no, no, no, no."

Sterling groans beside me. "You've got to be kidding me."

The silence is deafening. There are no gears turning, and no hum of machinery. Just the haunting sound of the wind howling through the trees below. My fingers ache from how hard I'm gripping the bar now.

"They fix this kind of thing, like, right away, right?"

"Usually, if there's someone still working the ski lift," he says, too calm. "Stop worrying. They'll get it moving again in a few minutes."

"W-what if it's hours?" My voice pitches higher. "What if they shut it down and forgot we're out here? We'll freeze. We'll starve. We'll—"

"Maisy." He turns toward me, voice firm enough to cut through my panic. "Breathe."

I suck in a shaky breath, but the lift sways and I freeze again. My legs already feel numb, and my heart is slamming against my ribs like it's trying to beat its way out.

Sterling sighs as he rips off one glove and digs in his jacket pocket. "Alright, hold on. I'll call Levi and tell him we're stuck."

Hope surges in my chest until I see the look on his face when he stares down at his phone.

"Please tell me it's ringing," I whisper.

He shows me the screen and there's no call...because there's no service.

My hands shake. "Oh my God. We're going to be stuck up here all night. We're probably going to freeze to death for real."

"Maisy, stop." His tone is infuriatingly steady. "You're moving too much, and you're going to rock the lift and send us both plunging to our deaths."

I freeze instantly, gripping the bar with all my strength. "Why would you even say that?" I hiss through chattering teeth, not because I'm cold but because of the adrenaline coursing through my body.

"Because it's true." His mouth quirks, like he's trying not to laugh at my horror. "So quit squirming, sit still, and practice your breathing."

I glare at him, but it's hard to hold onto anger when my heart's racing this fast. My chest feels tight, like there's no room for air, and I'm certain I'm about to have a full-blown meltdown.

Sterling must notice because he nudges my knee with his. "Hey, don't spiral. Levi will realize we never made it down, and I'm sure he'll send someone back to the lift tower to run a loop. Worst case, we're just waiting an hour or so."

"An hour?" I squeak.

He grins now. "Better than all night, right?"

I groan and press my forehead to the back of my gloved hands. "I hate you," I mutter.

The chair rocks again with the wind, and I swear my soul leaves my body.

"This is it," I mutter again, gripping the bar tighter. "This is how I die. Frozen solid on a ski lift with my ex-boyfriend, of all people. They'll find my body months from now, icicles hanging from my nose."

Sterling chuckles under his breath. "Wow. Dramatic." He gives me a slow applause. "And what do you mean 'of all people?' I'm probably the best person for you to be stranded with."

I snap my head toward him. "And why's that?"

He shrugs, but I don't miss the smirk pulling at the corner of his mouth. "I can help keep you warm."

"How?" I ask, arching a brow as I finally turn my head to look at him.

He looks at me now, his eyes sparkling with the suggestion he isn't saying out loud, and I press my thighs tighter together to stop the dull needy ache that's building in my core. I can't let him know that my body still wants him. So I do what I do best. I shut it down.

"First of all, ew. Second of all, we're dangling hundreds of feet in the air on what's basically a metal lawn chair strung up by a glorified clothesline!"

"It's not a clothesline, Maisy." His lips twitch like he's fighting a smile. "It's a steel cable. Made to hold, I don't know, way more weight than your five-foot-nothing frame is putting on it."

"Five-foot-three," I bite back.

"Sure." He smirks. "On a good day and in boots."

I jab him in the side with my elbow, and to my horror, the chair sways again. I let out a squeak, gripping his arm like my life depends on it.

Sterling's laugh rings out, warm and rich in the freezing air. "Okay, okay. Stop moving before you actually do send us crashing."

"I hate you," I say again, glaring at him as I rip my hands away from him, but my heart is hammering too hard for me to really mean it.

His voice grows soft. "No, you don't."

Something in my chest twists and I open my mouth to fire back, but the words get stuck in my throat, forcing the silence to press in again.

I risk a glance at him, noticing how close he's sitting, heat radiating from his body even through all the layers between us. His dark eyes catch mine again, and suddenly it feels like the whole world has narrowed to just us in this chair.

"You're still the worst," I whisper, noticing how softly I say it.

His lips curve, but it's not quite a smile. "So I've been told."

The air between us grows charged, and my breath fogs in front of me. For a fleeting, terrifying moment, I forget all about the lift. His gaze pins me in place, the only thing I can focus on as the silence stretches. My pulse is pounding so loud that I swear he must hear it.

The lift creaks again, swaying with the wind, and it breaks whatever spell we were under. I look away, shivering as I feel the cold creep in. Sterling notices, and without a word, he digs into his pocket and pulls out two hand warmers. He cracks them, shakes them, then holds them out toward me.

"Here. Put these in your gloves."

I fumble, pulling my gloves off with my teeth so I can grab the warmers and stuff them inside, but somehow both gloves slip and plunge for the snowy mountain below us. We both watch as they tumble in slow motion, bouncing once against the metal bar before plummeting into the snowy darkness below.

"Shit." My voice is loud in the silence. "That was my favorite pair."

For a moment, neither of us say anything. We're both staring down at the spot where my gloves disappeared.

Sterling sighs, then, to my surprise, he yanks his own gloves off and stuffs the warmers inside. Before I can protest, he's shoving them onto my hands.

"Sterling—"

"Don't start." His tone is final as he tugs the second one snug around my wrist and my hands explode in warmth.

"But your hands will freeze—"

"I'll be fine." He cuts me off again, his jaw tight, eyes turned away, scanning the darkness surrounding us like the cold doesn't even bother him. His bare hands disappear into his jacket pockets.

I stare at him, at the stubborn set of his shoulders, at the way he pretends this isn't costing him anything, and my throat feels tight.

"Sterling..." I whisper, softer this time.

He finally looks at me, and the weight of his gaze nearly knocks the air from my lungs. His eyes are searching, and too familiar. It's too much, but I don't want it to stop.

The space between us shrinks without either of us moving, and my breath clouds the air, mingling with his. The chair creaks again, swaying, but neither of us looks away this time.

It would be so easy—too easy—to lean in and close that tiny gap. I can almost remember how his lips felt on mine. His gaze drops, just for a heartbeat, to my mouth, and my pulse trips as I realize he's probably thinking the same thing.

Sterling starts to lean in, and I'm prepared for it, but the lift jolts back to life and jerks us forward with a loud groan. I gasp, grabbing the safety bar to steady myself, and the spell shatters once more.

Sterling clears his throat, turning his face away as if nothing happened. "Told you it wouldn't be all night."

But my heart's still pounding, and I can't convince myself it's not because of him.

THE CHAIR EASES into the docking bay at the bottom, the lights of the resort glowing warm against the dark mountains. My legs feel shaky when my boots hit the ground, but I keep my chin up, refusing to let Sterling see.

Of course, Levi's already waiting. Leaning casually on his board, grinning at us.

"Well, well." His eyes jump from me to Sterling and back again. "Thought you two got eaten by a yeti or something. I'm surprised Maisy didn't scream the whole mountain down when the lift stopped."

My jaw drops. "Did you stop it on purpose?"

He doesn't say anything but the devilish smirk on his face is answer enough. "Did you two get some good bonding time in?" Levi asks, stepping between me and Sterling and resting his arms on our shoulders as we start walking. "Are you two finally friends again?"

Friends.

"I don't know that we can ever be friends," Sterling mutters under his breath, loud enough for me to hear, and it hurts to hear.

"Of course you can." Levi laughs, clapping Sterling on the shoulder. "Anyway, you're both coming to Lodge Night. No excuses. Everyone's heading down to the staff lounge for dinner and drinks. It'll be super chill."

I open my mouth to decline, but Levi barrels on. "Sterling, you'll love it too. It's a good crew. You've been gone too long, man."

Sterling looks like he's about to say no too, so I cut in first because I know how much my brother wants his best friend to come. "We'll be there."

Sterling shoots me a side-eye glare, but Levi nods in approval. "Perfect. Go get changed and meet me in the staff lounge. Maisy knows where it is."

He releases us and walks off toward the lodge, leaving me and Sterling in the quiet.

Sterling exhales through his nose, clearly annoyed. "Is there a reason you accepted the invite on my behalf?"

"Someone had to," I say, brushing past him toward the parking lot where my truck is. "You were about to chicken out."

SEVEN

STERLING

THE FAMILIAR SCENT of Maisy's fruity-floral perfume hits me straight away when I join her at the front door of the chalet, along with hundreds of memories of us. I'm not surprised she still wears it, it's been her signature scent for as long as I've known her, but it's been so long since I smelled anything remotely similar that it leaves an aching sadness in my chest that I have to literally rub away.

"Did you intentionally match with me, or?" she asks, eyeing me up and down as she reaches for her chocolate brown plaid coat that hangs on the metal hook.

I'm wearing a beige knit sweater and chocolate brown chinos, while she's wearing a matching beige chunky sweater and pants set. We always had similar tastes in fashion, but I just thought it was a side-effect of being a couple that spent almost all hours of the day together when we weren't working.

"I can change," I say, ready to run back to my room.

"No," she says quickly, stopping me mid-turn. "You look... good."

I can't help the cocky grin that spreads on my face as I turn

35

back around to face her. She rolls her eyes and sighs as soon as she sees my expression, snatching my coat off the hook and shoving it into my arms.

"Maisy Hart," I purr as I put my jacket on. "Was that a compliment?"

She ignores me as she stomps out of the house, and toward her truck. I let out a low chuckle as I follow her, locking the front door behind me.

"Do you still know how to drive?" she asks, turning to glare at me. "I assume you don't get much practice anymore in that beach town you're living in."

"Yes, Maisy. I still know how to drive," I deadpan. "Any more ridiculous questions?"

She fishes for something in her coat pocket before pulling out her keys and tossing them at me. I quickly snatch them before they hit the ground, looking at her in confusion.

"Good," she says, rounding the truck to the passenger's side. "Because I plan on drinking tonight so you'll need to drive us home."

Maisy drinking?

That's new.

THE STAFF LOUNGE is huge and packed full of unfamiliar faces. It smells faintly like roast beef, melted cheese, and alcohol. The low lights bounce off the wooden beams, creating a cozy vibe along with the crackling fireplace in the far corner of the room.

"Glad you two made it," Levi says as he approaches us with a too-wide grin, and I force my own half-smile in return.

I'm not one for big social events and Levi knows that, but I'll bear through it tonight, especially if Maisy is planning on drinking. I'll need to keep an eye on her. Levi takes mine and Maisy's coat before tossing them on a nearby overflowing coat rack, and she walks off without a word toward the bar at the back of the room.

I silently watch her go until Levi nudges me with his elbow. "You good?" he asks, studying me.

Fuck, caught staring at his sister.

"When did your sister start drinking?" I ask, trying to sound nonchalant as his gaze follows her to the bar.

We watch her hold up two fingers before the server slides her two shots of something brown, and she throws it back down her throat right away. It's weird seeing the girl that used to hate alcohol drink it so easily tonight.

"Shortly after...everything," he says, watching her with a slight frown as she orders another two.

"You mean the accident?"

"And the breakup." His eyes find mine. "Come on, there's a bunch of people I want to introduce you to."

It feels like someone landed a sucker punch straight to my stomach. Maisy started drinking after we broke up? She seemed so sure about not wanting to continue our relationship. Was it all an act? Did I buy into all the bullshit she said to me?

Fuck. Maybe I did.

It's been thirty minutes of Levi introducing me to his new friends as "*The* Sterling I always tell you about." They all greet me like we're longtime friends, but I've never seen these people in my life. Some of them say they remember me from high school, but those days are all a blur. All I remember from those years is Maisy.

Speaking of, she's tucked away in some corner with a guy I

haven't met yet, and I can tell she's nowhere near sober. I sip my beer as I watch her flirt with him, twirling her hair around her fingers while she looks up at him with her big blue eyes. I try convincing myself it's nothing, but I keep finding my gaze snapping back to her.

"Who's that?" I ask Levi, keeping my voice casual.

Levi follows my line of sight, eyebrows lifting. "Oh, that's just Jeff."

I choke a little on my beer. "As in 'rental shop' Jeff?"

Levi nods. "Yeah. How'd you know?"

"Maisy mentioned him once. He helped her get her gear."

"I don't really like the guy," he says, gaze darkening as he watches Jeff touch Maisy's shoulder while he laughs at something she said.

That makes two of us, buddy.

"Why not?" I take another sip from my beer, but my eyes stay glued on Maisy.

"He's been trying to get into my sister's pants for over a year now."

I grit my teeth, focusing on my beer and trying to calm myself down. It's not like she's mine anymore. I know that. But I can't fight off the jealousy in my chest as I watch Jeff lean in slightly, and brush a strand of hair behind her ear.

"And I'm guessing there's a reason you don't want him getting that close to your sister?" I turn my gaze to Levi.

He nods. "He's already sleeping around with two other girls on payroll, and neither of them knows it. I'm not about to let him play around with my sister too."

He stands up and clears his throat before calling out to Jeff to come over. I watch as Jeff's attention leaves Maisy, and he takes a cautious step back when he realizes Levi can see him.

Pussy.

He starts to walk toward us, and I look at Maisy as she

follows behind him, but she's already watching me. I can practically see her catch the tension in my jaw. Her lips twitch into a tiny amused smirk, and it's maddening.

I stand up next to Levi as Jeff approaches, sip my beer again, and force a casual mask over the jealousy curling in my chest.

Keep it together, Sterling.

"Sterling, meet Jeff," Levi says. "He's the guy that runs our rental shop most days."

Jeff extends a hand, and I shake it hard enough to assert dominance without it being obvious to anyone watching. "So you're the guy that almost killed Maisy."

Nearby conversations die down as people start listening in, and Jeff lets out a nervous laugh as he releases my hand.

"What do you mean?" he asks nervously.

"You sized her bindings wrong." Jeff blinks, surprised, and I let my smirk do the rest. "She's lucky I caught it before she actually hit the slope. Could've caused a serious injury, Jason."

Maisy watches the exchange, eyes flicking between us, and I swear she's amused by my little jab, but that doesn't help the knot twisting in my chest.

"It's Jeff," he says quietly, but I pretend not to hear him as I pat his shoulder a little too firmly, my jaw set.

"Is that true?" Levi asks, looking pissed at Jeff.

Maisy doesn't say anything, as she narrows her eyes at me, which doesn't exactly help Jeff's case.

"Honest mistake, boss," Jeff finally says.

"That type of mistake could cost someone their life," Levi says through clenched teeth. "It could have cost my sister her life."

"But," Maisy finally speaks as she steps toward Levi and places her hands on his arms, "it didn't, and now Jeff knows to triple check things before releasing guests to the mountain. Right, Jeff?"

Jeff freezes for half a beat, and then nods frantically before excusing himself. Levi watches him go with a pissed off expression before looking down at his sister, just as angry.

"You shouldn't have let him off so easily," he mutters as she releases his arms.

"It was either that or let you beat the shit out of him, which I could already see you getting ready to do, hothead."

Levi scoffs, looking away. "He'd deserve it."

As much as Levi likes to tease his sister, she's his entire world. With lawyer parents as busy as theirs, all they had was each other while growing up.

"Let's go get a drink together," Maisy suggests, already steering Levi toward the bar.

He stops and turns to look at me. "You coming?"

I shake my head and hold up my beer bottle. "I'm good."

But that doesn't stop my eyes from tracking her every movement as the night goes on. She laughs too easily, and I can feel that old pull, that familiarity that used to make everything feel effortless.

I make a mental note to keep my distance for the rest of my time here, hiding my irritation with a practiced smirk, because apparently, this is my life now—keeping her safe, keeping my hands to myself, and gritting my teeth while watching her flirt.

HOURS LATER, Levi is laughing with a group near the bar, Maisy is probably off somewhere with Jeff again, and I don't want to get caught in any more of the lodge's endless small talk. It's time to excuse myself.

I make my way through the crowd, weaving past people, and just as I reach the coat rack, I bump into someone—Maisy.

"Sterling?" Her cheeks are flushed from the alcohol she's been drinking. "Are you leaving?"

"Yeah," I reply, trying to keep my tone casual, but I'm still jealous as hell after watching her flirt with Jeff earlier, even though I have no right to be.

Her eyebrows lift. "You weren't even going to tell me? We're supposed to go back together."

I shrug, letting out a humourless laugh. "I thought your brother could just drive you back...or Jason. Don't want to ruin your night by going home early."

She doesn't respond as she tilts her head, studying me like she's trying to read my mind.

I sigh, rubbing the back of my neck. "Are you coming home with me, Mais?" I let the nickname slip naturally, without thinking.

Her eyes widen for a fraction of a second, and I swear I see that tough exterior finally giving way.

"Yeah," she says.

I give a small nod, allowing a subtle relief to settle over me as we step out into the cold mountain air biting at my cheeks. I lead the way to where we parked the truck earlier, the soft glow of the lodge fading behind us. Even if the night has been messy, complicated, and full of tension, right now, I've got her by my side. And for tonight, knowing she's with me instead of Jeff, is enough.

EIGHT

MAISY

I'VE NEVER NOTICED how winding the road that leads to the chalet is. Every bend feels too sudden to be safe, but Sterling drives carefully while the snow falls around us. I sit with my body facing the window, pretending to focus on the snowy trees even though they're barely visible. Really, I'm just trying not to sway in my seat and give away how tipsy I feel.

I'm not drunk, just warm in the face, a little floaty, my thoughts slower than normal, and I've been concentrating on breathing evenly so Sterling doesn't notice.

He hasn't said a word since we left the lodge. His jaw flexes every so often as if he's biting back everything he wants to say. I almost tell him to spit it out, but he beats me to it.

"Why'd you start drinking?" His eyes don't leave the road. "You used to hate that stuff."

My stomach knots, because of all the questions he could've asked, of course it had to be that one.

I force a laugh, brittle around the edges. "That's what you've been brooding over this whole drive?"

His hand tightens on the steering wheel. "Maisy." All he

42

says is my name, but it's enough to send a shiver down my spine.

I glance out the window again, the trees whipping past. "People change," I say quietly. "Things change."

"That's not an answer."

I bite my lip, heat prickling behind my eyes. He doesn't get it—he wasn't here. He didn't see the mess I was after the accident. After us. He got to run away to his surf town while I was stuck here trying to pick up the pieces of myself.

I swallow hard, throat tight. "Maybe I just needed something to take the edge off," I murmur, more to the glass than to him.

The only sound is the hum of the engine for a few minutes before he speaks. "You don't need that," he says softly.

The words slam into me, both comforting and infuriating, because they sound so much like the old Sterling—the one who always thought he could fix me, even when I didn't want fixing.

I turn toward him, my voice more aggressive than I mean it to be. "You don't get to tell me what I need."

His jaw works, but he keeps his eyes on the road, knuckles white on the steering wheel, and the silence returns heavier than before.

By the time Sterling pulls into the driveway of the chalet, the silence between us is so thick I can barely breathe. The headlights sweep over the wooden beams and dark windows, snow piled high along the edges of the porch.

He kills the engine, the hum dying into stillness, and for a long moment neither of us moves. My seatbelt presses against my chest like a restraint, keeping me in place when every nerve in me feels strung tight.

Sterling finally unclips his belt, then glances at me. "Do you need help to get inside?"

The question is so simple, but the way his eyes search mine

makes it feel like something else entirely. Like he's peeling me open, waiting for me to admit what I don't want to say.

That I need him.

I shake my head too quickly, fumbling with my buckle. "I'm fine."

I push the door open, cold air rushing in, but his hand comes down lightly on my arm before I can get out. Not hard, or possessive, but enough to make my heart pound.

"Maisy." He says my name like a warning and a plea all at once.

I turn back to him, and suddenly we're too close in the dark cab of the truck, heat rolling between us despite the cool winter air just outside. His hand lingers on my arm, and his eyes drop to my mouth, just for a heartbeat, before he drags them back up to mine.

Every muscle in me goes still. One move, one breath the wrong way, and I'd lean across the console and taste him again. I want to. God, I want to. But I don't. And neither does he.

His hand falls away, leaving a ghost of heat in its place as he clears his throat, pushing his door open. "Come on. It's late."

I swing my door open and jump out, regretting it instantly when I slip on a patch of ice and land on my ass with an *oomph*. Turns out I'm definitely not just tipsy, I'm drunk as a skunk.

"Maisy?" Sterling's worried voice calls out as he rushes to round the truck. "Are you hurt?"

I groan, embarrassed. "Just my pride," I mutter as he helps me to my feet, and suddenly we're too close again.

My palms rest on his chest as he holds me steady by my arms, and I'm looking up into his deep brown eyes that are only inches away from my face. Maybe it's the alcohol, but every reason for why I shouldn't kiss him right now escapes me, and I reach up cupping his cheeks as I stand up on my tiptoes to reach his mouth.

But before I can make contact, he pulls his face out of my hands and releases my arms, taking a step back, clearing his throat. The mortification hits me instantly, and I know I'm beet red as I look at him confused, dropping back down to the balls of my feet.

"Right, well I'm going to go inside and cry myself to sleep," I say, flashing him a forced smile as I turn to run inside.

Sterling grabs onto my elbow, stopping me from getting far. "Maisy, just wait a second," he says, his voice gently pleading.

"Why should I?" I ask, my embarrassment turning into anger.

He lets out a deep sigh as his eyes search mine. "I didn't step back because I don't want to kiss you. Trust me, it's all I can think about. But you made it very clear three years ago, to me and to your brother, that you and I are done."

I almost interrupt him, but he gives me a look that has me biting the insides of my cheeks to keep my mouth shut as he continues.

"I don't know if this is how you normally get when you've been drinking, because this is my first time being around you when you're like this, so I don't want to let you do anything you might regret in the morning. I don't want to take advantage of the situation. I don't want to take advantage of you."

As angry as I want to be, his reasoning for rejecting me is sweet and such a Sterling answer that I can't stay mad at him.

I nod calmly. "I'm sorry, you're probably right. Let's just go inside so I can sleep this off."

He lets my arm go, sliding his hands into his pockets as he studies me. "You're not still planning to cry yourself to sleep, are you?"

I give him a half-grin and turn. "Maybe just one lone tear," I say over my shoulder as I head inside.

I hear him chuckle low behind me. "Don't waste your tears on me, Mais."

Mais.

That's the second time he's called me that, and hearing that old nickname makes my eyes sting. He doesn't know that I still cry myself to sleep some nights when I think about him. About how I pushed him away. About how I woke up one day only to find out he actually left, not just me, but the town. About how I was forced to hear the rumours of him physically moving on with other girls too, while I was here unable to even think about moving on without feeling physically sick.

It's been one slow heartbreak after another when it comes to Sterling, but I won't let him know that. He'd beat himself up over that knowledge and it wouldn't be fair to him.

He had every right to move on.

Even if I can't.

NINE

STERLING

MAISY IS DIFFERENT TODAY. We're back on the mountain for another lesson, but instead of the snappy, sarcastic Maisy that I'm used to, she's quiet. I want to believe her when she says it's just the hangover, but I know her well enough to know it's because of what happened between us when we got home last night.

She went in for a kiss, and honestly if she hadn't been drinking, I would've let her. I would've pulled her body flush against mine and poured everything I had into that kiss. I'd show her just how much I want her. How much I never stopped wanting her.

But I'm not like that.

I won't take advantage of someone who isn't sober enough to make smart decisions. And after everything Maisy said when she broke up with me three years ago, kissing me definitely wouldn't have been a smart decision.

"Oof!" Maisy falls back onto her ass, snapping my attention back to our lesson.

47

"Ready to try again?" I ask after she's pushed herself back up. "You're not distributing your weight enough."

She lets out a frustrated growl and rips off her gloves, the ones I gave her, and throws them to the snow.

"This shouldn't be so hard!" I walk over to the gloves and bend down to pick them up. "I'm a pro skier, my brother runs a god-damn ski lodge, and I've been surrounded by snowboarders my entire life. This should be easy for me."

I stay crouched, staring down at the gloves as I try to find the right words.

"It doesn't matter that you're a pro at a similar sport, or that your brother owns a ski lodge, or that you've been surrounded by snowboarders your entire life," I say, standing up and walking over to her. "You're still learning something new, and learning a new skill isn't supposed to be easy. That's what makes it feel so rewarding when you finally get it right, Mais."

She doesn't say anything as I gently take her hands and slide the gloves back onto them, but I see the fire return to her eyes and I know my words resonated with her.

"Let's go again, and I'll guide you this time. Okay?"

She nods and gets into position, still making the same error as before. I walk over to the board I brought for this lesson, clipping my boot into it, and sliding the board over to where she is before clipping my other boot in once I'm behind her.

Gently, I reach over and place my hands on either side of her waist, feeling her tense instantly.

"Relax your body," I say, waiting until she listens before I correct her posture. "Let's try and carve down to the green flag all the way down there."

She gives me a short nod and we start, my hands on her waist the whole time. I feel her shifting her weight early and then late as we move into the curve of the carve together, but I correct her each time and slowly she begins to do it herself.

"There you go," I say, unable to keep the pride out of my voice as she does a perfect carve when I let go. "You're doing it!"

No sooner are the words out of my mouth before she falls, not giving me enough time to avoid her. I fall on top of her, catching myself before my face collides with hers.

"I'm so sorry," she whispers, her big blue eyes staring up at mine.

"We've really got to stop finding ourselves in this position," I say with a grin. "Someone might report us to your brother for inappropriate mountain behaviour."

I expect her to snap at me for being obnoxious, but instead, Maisy does something that absolutely catches me off guard.

She hits me with a snowball.

"You did not just do that," I say, watching as she tries to bite back a grin of her own.

I reach back, unclip my boots from my board, and sit up on my knees.

"I hate to break it to you but—"

I don't let her finish as I throw a snowball directly at her face. Her mouth drops open, and she stares at me shocked before I see the glimmer of competitiveness sparkle in her eyes.

"Maisy," I say in a warning tone as I stand to my feet, watching as she unclips her boots from the board. "Maisy, you don't want to do this."

"Do what, exactly?" she asks innocently while gathering a pile of snow and shaping it into a ball.

"You know that your aim sucks," I taunt, grabbing my own handful of snow and shaping it fast.

I watch her twist to the side and rear her arm back before she whips the snowball directly at my head. I duck just as it whizzes over my helmet.

What the fuck?

I slowly stand, jaw on the ground as I stare at her smirking back at me. "Correction," Maisy says, picking up another handful of snow. "My aim *sucked*. Past tense."

She throws another one, and this time it hits me square in the shoulder. I whip mine at her, but she jumps out of the way just before it hits her.

"Okay, Hart." I nod, feeling the competitiveness flare to life inside of me as I gather more snow. "You're on."

"Have you no shame?" Levi says, his tone annoyed as he escorts me and Maisy away from the ski hill. "I can't believe I got called by the ski patrol because my best friend, who's an instructor at this resort might I remind you, and my sister were having a military grade snowball fight."

"Maisy started it," I mutter as he takes both of our boards along with my ski-lift pass.

"Did not," she argues, narrowing her eyes at me.

"I don't care who started it," Levi says, giving us both a stern look. "No more boarding for the day. I'll give these back to you two tomorrow. Tonight, I want you guys to think about what is and isn't acceptable mountain behaviour."

"Yes, *Dad*," Maisy salutes Levi before walking off.

"I hate when she calls me that," he mutters to me, watching as she goes. "Especially when she knows she did something wrong."

"Don't worry," I say, patting his shoulder. "It won't happen again."

He sighs, tearing his eyes away from her and looking at me. "Keep an eye on her, alright? I don't want her doing anything reckless with all this free time."

Reckless? That doesn't sound like Maisy. But I just nod and wave him off as I jog to catch up to her.

"Wait up," I say just before reaching her. "I need to go to the gear shop for a sec before we head back to the chalet. Want to come with me?"

She stops walking and turns her head to look at me. "You want me to come shopping with you?"

"Yeah." I nod. "I do."

"Okay."

"So what exactly are we looking for here?" Maisy asks, skimming the racks of multicoloured goggles.

"New gloves for you."

That grabs her attention, and she spins to look at me. "What's wrong with the ones I'm using now?"

I try and fail to bite back my smirk as she follows me to the wall of gloves.

"Well, for starters, they're mine." I see the faintest pink creep onto her cheeks. "And I'm sorry to inform you that it's very obvious they are too big for your hands."

"Right," she says, drawing out the word.

She turns her attention to the gloves for a few minutes before settling on a pink pair identical to the ones she lost. I take them from her hands and walk over to the cashier, paying for them quickly before she has a chance to pull her credit card out of her wallet.

"I could've paid," she mumbles, taking the new gloves from me.

"I know," I reply, watching as she removes my gloves and hands them back to me before sliding on her new pair. "How do they feel?"

"Like they fit." She shrugs, but I don't miss the longing look she gives mine as I slide them into my jacket pocket.

TEN

MAISY

STERLING WAS NEVER much of a cook when we were together three years ago. Back then, he could burn water without even trying. His idea of a balanced meal was anything microwavable, paired with a sports drink.

Who knew that in three years, he'd not only learned how to cook, but he'd learned how to cook *well*. Better than well actually—tonight's dinner, roast beef on mashed potatoes, is Michelin Star level, but I'll never admit it to him.

I expect him to retreat to his room after dinner the way he usually does, but tonight he decides to stay in the living room with me. I'm curled up on the couch under my blanket, reading a cozy holiday romcom while the fireplace crackles. It's my nightly me-time.

Sterling ruins it when he drops down on the cushion beside me, close enough for the couch to dip. His cologne drifts over—clean, and woodsy, and distracting as hell. I breathe through the distraction of his scent while I reread the same line for the fourth time, but all hope is lost when he reaches over and snatches half of the blanket off of me and onto himself instead.

I snap my book shut and glare at him. "I was using that."

He doesn't even glance at me, thumbs tapping away on his phone. "Oh, were you?"

"Yes," I grind out, tugging the blanket back over myself.

Without missing a beat, Sterling pulls it right back. I let out a frustrated growl as I sit up straighter, tossing my book onto the nearby side table.

"What's your issue?"

He smirks faintly, eyes still on his screen. "Well, for starters, you've got a real sharing problem."

"I don't have to share if I don't want to," I snap. "It's called boundaries. I'm not here to people please."

That gets his attention. He drops his phone, tugging more of the blanket his way. "Funny. You used to love pleasing me. "

My mouth falls open. *Oh, he did not just say that.*

"Is that what you thought?" I shoot back, smirking now. "Yikes."

His brows knit as he tries to decode my meaning, and I take advantage of the distraction to wrench the blanket free and bolt. My heart races as I dash toward the hallway that leads to my bedroom, clutching the blanket to my chest.

If he won't let me have it in peace, then he doesn't get it at all.

As I reach the hallway, I hear the heavy thud of his footsteps chasing me. I glance back just in time to see six-foot-something Sterling charging, and a half-laugh, half-scream escapes me as I sprint for my bedroom.

I don't make it.

Strong hands catch me, spinning me around. My back hits the wall, and my arms are pinned above my head in one swift move. The blanket drops uselessly to the floor as his body presses against mine, heat radiating off him as his chest rises and falls in time with mine.

"I don't think it's the blanket you wanted," he murmurs, voice low and rough, vibrating through me where his chest brushes mine.

My lips part, ready to snap something back, but nothing comes out. His smirk deepens at my silence, eyes studying mine like he's reading every thought I'm desperately trying to hide.

"You know exactly what you're doing," he says, leaning in just enough that his breath ghosts over my cheek. "Starting fights. Running away. Making me chase you. I know you, Maisy, so don't pretend this isn't what you wanted."

Heat floods my body, but I force out a laugh, deflecting. "Wow, you really do have an ego problem."

His grip on my wrists tightens, not painfully, but firm enough to remind me I'm not going anywhere unless he allows it. "Ego? No," he says, eyes dark and unflinching. "I have clarity. I know when you're lying—even to yourself."

My stomach flips at that, my heartbeat pounding hundreds of miles an hour against my ribs like it's trying to escape. His face is so close I can see the tiny scar along his jawline, the one I used to trace with my fingertip.

"This—" his voice dips as he presses in closer, pinning me harder against the wall, "—is exactly where you wanted me. Exactly where you want to be."

I try to shake my head, to deny it, but the movement is weak, unconvincing even to myself. His eyes burn into mine, catching every moment of hesitation.

"You could push me off right now," he adds, softer this time, almost a dare. "But you won't."

The words steal my breath. I hate how right he is. I hate how my body arches closer instead of away, how my pulse quickens when his thumb brushes lightly over the inside of my wrist.

"Sterling..." I whisper, though I don't even know if it's meant as a warning or a plea.

He grins, slow and devastating, dipping his head until his lips hover over mine. Close enough that I can taste his breath, feel the warmth radiating off him.

"Say it," he murmurs, eyes locked on my mouth. "Admit you wanted this."

My throat works, but the words refuse to form. My silence is answer enough.

The tension between us crackles dangerously, every second stretching like a wire pulled taut. If either of us moves, it'll snap.

But we don't.

We just stand there, caught between resistance and surrender, hearts racing, breaths colliding, until the only thing I know for sure is that he's right. This is exactly what I wanted.

Slowly, I tilt my chin up to close the small distance between us. My heart pounds even harder as his breath brushes mine, my lips parting, ready to taste him. But the shrill sound of my phone shatters the moment, ricocheting through the hall.

I jolt, but Sterling doesn't move. His grip is iron-tight as one hand still holds my wrists above my head, while the other slides down the curve of my back and down my ass with practiced ease, plucking my phone out of my back pocket.

He looks down at the name flashing on my screen, and his gaze darkens, jaw flexing as he looks from my phone back to me. I watch as he swipes to answer and raises it to his ear.

"Jeff," he says, eyes locked on mine the whole time. "What can I do for you?"

His tone is controlled, but he can't hide the annoyance from his expression as he listens for a beat.

"No, this isn't Maisy. It's Sterling."

Another pause.

"Yeah, we live together."

My stomach drops. It's not technically a lie. We *are* living together for the next month in this chalet. But he and I both know that's not how Jeff will take it. But if I'm being honest, do I really care how Jeff takes it?

"Sure. We'll both be there tomorrow." Without waiting for a reply, he ends the call and lowers the phone, taking his time sliding it back into my pocket as his fingers deliberately brush over the curve of my hip.

Once my phone is back in place, he finally releases my wrists and steps back just enough to let me breathe again.

"Your boyfriend invited us to the Winter Festival tomorrow night," he says, voice maddeningly casual.

"He's not my boyfriend," I say, too quickly.

"Mmm," is all he says.

He slides his hands into his pant pockets and strolls back toward the living room, leaving me pressed against the wall, breathless and flushed. The blanket lies abandoned at my feet, but I can't seem to move, not with the echo of his hands still burning through me.

ELEVEN

STERLING

MAISY and I weave through the crowd at the Bluewater Bluffs Winter Festival. The air is thick with the smell of roasted chestnuts, cinnamon, and pine trees. String lights are strung everywhere, glowing against the icy night, and a group of carolers are singing somewhere near the town square. It feels like we're walking straight through a holiday movie set, and I hate to admit it, but I've kind of missed this.

When we were younger, it was a tradition for me, Levi, and Maisy to go to the Winter Festival together. We mostly went because Levi and Maisy's parents wouldn't let her go alone and I would tag along to put Levi out of his misery.

When Maisy and I started dating, I relieved Levi of the duty altogether, but I always found it boring. Until now.

When Jeff first waves us over to his group of friends, I expect Maisy to gravitate to his side and laugh at his stupid jokes the way she did at the dinner the other night. But instead, she gives him a polite smile, says hi, and stays by my side. I can't hold back the smug grin when Jeff's eyes land on mine.

The crowd grows thicker as we follow the group, and I

open my arm for Maisy to take. She grabs ahold of my bicep and it's not long before we stop to watch a violinist play on the street, Jeff's group continuing on without us.

"Let's go to that café," Maisy says, pointing to a decorated coffee shop down the street.

Before I can answer, she pulls me down the cobbled street. I open the door for her, hearing the chime of a bell as we step in. Inside, the café is cozy, wooden beams crisscrossing along the ceiling, and a crackling fire surrounded by plush cushions.

Maisy releases my arms, rushing to the glass display near the counter. I'm not surprised when I find her staring at the platter of cranberry brie bites—her favourite.

"Welcome to Sunrise Café, would you like to try the brie bites?" a smiling redhead says from across the counter.

"I'd like them all please," Maisy says.

I almost choke as I quickly count at least twenty brie bites on the platter, the redhead looking just as surprised. She doesn't question it though as she gets to packing up all twenty of them.

"Would you like anything to drink?" she asks, as she rings up the brie bites.

Maisy turns her big blue eyes on me. "What's that drink you always used to get?"

"Mulled cider?"

She snaps her fingers. "Yes! That's the one."

"But that has alc—" I pause, remembering that she drinks now. "Make that two mulled ciders, please," I say, pulling my wallet out.

"Is that for here or to go?" the redhead asks nervously.

Why is she nervous?

"Uhm..." I glance around, my eyes landing on a booth in the back corner of the café. "Let's do here."

The redhead freezes as she follows my gaze to the booth.

Then she takes a deep breath, turns her attention back to me, and pins me with knitted brows.

"Alright, but no funny business back there, okay?"

I rear my head back, my brows furrowing. "What does that mean?"

She lets out another deep breath, looking between Maisy and me before leaning forward, making sure no one else can hear what she's saying.

"Just over a year ago, I had a couple sit in that very booth and they...they did stuff that you shouldn't do in public."

Maisy gasps, eating up the smalltown gossip.

I, on the other hand, roll my eyes as I pay and take my mulled cider from her. "Like what, making out?"

I bring the cup to my lips and take a sip as she shakes her head. "No, the guy was fingering his girl right in that booth!"

I choke on my drink, sputtering as I cough, my eyes going round. "The hell?"

"I know!" she exclaims. "And what makes it worse is he paid me off before leaving to make sure I didn't tell the local paper. Apparently, he's some big hot-shot surfer from Saltwater Springs."

Maisy's eyes instantly snap to mine and I mirror her shocked expression as the redhead taps her chin deep in thought.

"I think his name was Gerald," she says before frowning. "Or was it Pipin?"

"You don't mean Griffin, do you?" I ask slowly.

She snaps her fingers together. "That's the name!"

"You know him?" Maisy asks.

I look between the two women, disturbed with this new knowledge and not wanting to continue this conversation any longer.

"No. I just heard the name before," I say abruptly, handing

Maisy her drink before grabbing the bag of brie bites. "On second thought, I think we'll actually just take everything to-go. Thanks again."

I rush out of there, Maisy in tow, and as soon as the café door closes behind us, Maisy turns to look at me.

"You definitely know Griffin," she says, narrowing her eyes as she studies me.

"Take a sip of your drink," I deflect, trying to distract her.

The last thing I want to be talking about is Griffin Jones fingering his girlfriend, Eliana Ward.

I'm still not used to the idea of Maisy drinking. She was always so strict with her diet because of all the hard work she was putting in to get into the Olympics. But I guess now that that's done with, it makes sense she'd want to try all the things she missed out on back then.

I watch as she slowly lifts the cup to her lips. She blows on it carefully, then takes a sip, closing her eyes like she's savoring it.

Her hum of approval punches straight through my chest. "That's way too good. I can't believe I was missing out on this all these years."

"I'll buy you another one on the way out if you want more," I say before I can stop myself.

Her smile curves slowly, but she doesn't say anything as she reaches for one of the brie bites in the bag. We walk back to the main street, ciders in hand, wandering through the market stalls strung with fairy lights. She pauses to admire handmade ornaments, knitted scarves, and sugar-dusted pastries. I buy her one of those stupid oversized gingerbread cookies shaped like a snowflake, mostly because she keeps staring at it but won't reach for her wallet.

She takes it from me, rolling her eyes. "You're ridiculous."

"And you're welcome," I shoot back, but the truth is, I like seeing her with it. I like seeing her with all of this—her cheeks pink, her dark hair sprinkled with snowflakes, and her laughing because of something I said. It reminds me of how things used to be, and I miss it.

We're surrounded by families and couples, people bundled in scarves and mittens, holding hands, leaning into each other. It should feel suffocating being here with my ex.

But it feels right. Like maybe this is how it should be.

We're still drifting between stalls, Maisy pointing at literally everything from carved wooden nutcrackers to jars of spiced honey, when Jeff suddenly materializes out of the crowd.

"There you are," he says, slipping into step beside her, way too close. "We're all headed to the rink. Are you guys coming?"

Maisy opens her mouth to answer for us, but I beat her to it.

"I'm good here," I say, calm but clipped. My fingers twitch, wanting to curl around her wrist, and pull her to me to create some distance between her and Jeff.

He blinks at me like I just spoke a foreign language, as if he can't understand why I answered his question instead of Maisy, before he looks back at her. "Do *you* want to skate?"

Maisy hesitates, then shakes her head, smiling politely. "Maybe another time. I kind of like wandering the markets."

Relief floods through me in waves, and I can't hold back my smug smile again when Jeff gives me a once-over, like he's sizing me up.

Jeff shrugs, trying to hide his disappointment. "Alright, suit yourself."

The moment he's gone, my jaw unclenches. I hadn't realized how tight I was holding it until now. The bastard pisses me off.

Maisy glances at me, brows lifted. "What was that?"

"What was what?" I ask, playing dumb as I take a long sip of my drink.

"I'm good here." She mocks me with a deep voice, lips pursed out as she does it.

"I don't sound like that." I roll my eyes. "Plus, you hate skating. I was just doing you a favour."

Maisy throws her head back and lets out a cackle, her eyes twinkling with amusement. "You don't like him, do you?"

I smirk. "Not when he looks at you the way he does."

She eyes me for a beat longer, like she wants to say something, but she lets it go, turning back to the stalls.

We wander farther down the line of stalls, until Maisy stops at a booth covered in glass ornaments—tiny hand-blown pieces that glitter under the bulbs. Snowflakes, reindeer, stars. She picks up one shaped like a pair of skis, turning it carefully in her hands.

Watching her holding the ornament jogs a memory. For as long as I've known Maisy, she's collected Christmas ornaments. She probably has a huge collection by now, but you can bet that every single piece has some sort of special meaning to her.

Her lips part slightly, like she's about to say something, but then she sets it back down and steps away. While she's looking at the chocolate selection they have, I grab the ornament and quickly pay for it before she notices.

The cashier catches on that I'm trying to be discreet and quickly places the ornament into a gift box, tying it with a bow as her eyes shift to make sure Maisy hasn't looked over yet. She slides the gift box over with a wink and I flash her a grateful grin before putting the box in my jacket pocket just as Maisy turns around.

"Ready to check out another booth?" I ask, doing my best to sound casual.

"Actually, I think I'm ready to head home."

My stomach plummets. "You want to go back already?" I

ask, feeling disappointed that the night is coming to an end already.

She nods. "I'm freezing, and honestly the only thing I can think about is the hot tub back at the chalet."

That grabs my attention, and I visibly straighten up. "There's a hot tub at the chalet?"

She nods, biting back her smirk. "Yeah, just outside the back doors. Want to join me?"

I clear my throat, trying to act normal while my dick has other ideas. Lucky for me, my jacket hides the tent it's pitching.

"Sure," I say, trying to sound casual. "Let's go."

TWELVE

MAISY

STERLING IS ALREADY OUTSIDE in the hot tub by the time I step into the bathroom to change because it took me twenty minutes to find the bikini I was looking for. I stare down at the bold, red fabric that borders on indecent.

I know the idea of both of us half-naked, close enough to touch, is a bad idea. We barely have any self-control around each other, and so much could happen if we're not careful. Going in the hot tub together is reckless. After all, I'm the one that decided to end things between us three years ago.

And still, I shimmy into the bikini, adjust the straps, and pull my robe over my shoulders, tying the belt tight around my waist before making my way outside.

The cold night air bites at my exposed ankles and face, stealing my breath. Snow covers the ground in glittering sheets, and the hot tub sits in the corner of the deck. Sterling is reclined against the side, one tanned arm draped over the edge. His brown curls damp from the steam, and his broad shoulders gleaming.

He looks up at the sound of the door closing behind me,

brown eyes locking on mine. They slowly move down to my robe, lingering a moment before rising back to my face with a look that makes my stomach flip. His silent way of telling me to take it off.

I slowly slip the robe off my shoulders, letting it fall to the ground in one swift movement. The cool air rushes over me, turning my skin a subtle shade of pink within seconds, while a shiver skates down my spine. The corner of his mouth ticks up, but I can see the way his throat works, the way his chest expands like he's fighting for control. I know that look better than anyone, and I know what I'm doing to him.

"Are you coming in or just planning to torture me?" he asks, his voice rough.

My lips curve. "Both."

I cross the deck, making a point to sway my hips more noticeably, and dip one foot in the hot tub. Sterling's gaze doesn't move as I lower myself beside him, water sloshing against my ribs. His thigh brushes mine under the surface, and I press just a little closer. I can feel the tension in his body, see the way he's gripping the edge of the tub, and a small, wicked part of me wants to see how far I can push him.

"Maisy," he warns, roughly, but there's no real force behind it.

"Sterling," I murmur back, tilting my head, and letting a teasing smile tug at my lips. My shoulder nudges his, and I watch him stiffen, jaw tight, and eyes darkening.

"Careful," he says again, voice almost a growl, and I can't hold back my grin.

I let my hands glide along the edge of the tub, slowly inching closer, lightly skimming my fingertips along his arm. I watch the subtle flex of his muscles, and the slight shift in his posture when our thighs press together again.

He's trying so hard to resist, I can tell, but I can also see the need that he's losing control over.

I dip my chest under the water for a moment, letting it ripple over my chest, then rise slowly, making sure he sees the water drip off my skin, the way my nipples pebble from the instant change in temperature.

"Maisy," he says again, firmer this time.

"Hmm?" I hum innocently, tilting my head, but my pulse is racing.

I lower my hand under the water, resting casually on the seat edge, close enough to his thigh to make the contact feel electric, and I let it linger there. He exhales sharply, the sound half agony half turned on.

"You're impossible," he mutters, eyes on me, but I don't look away.

"Am I?" I whisper, letting my voice drop low, with a teasing edge.

The way his jaw clenches is mesmerizing, and the slight dip of his chest as he swallows tells me he's right there on the edge, every inch aware of me. And yet he doesn't move closer, because he knows he shouldn't.

I know the rules, too. We're off-limits to each other now. We can be friends but nothing more. But friends don't look at friends the way Sterling is looking at me right now. Friends don't feel the things I feel when I'm around him.

My hand now trails a path up his leg and he catches my wrist lightly, just enough to stop my teasing, and I feel the electricity of his touch shoot straight through my arm. My heart starts to race, my chest tightens, my lips part slightly, and I know he feels it too.

"You know we can't," he murmurs, his lips grazing my wrist. "Your brother would kill us both."

The heat of his breath, the way his lips brush my skin, makes me shiver despite the water and I bite back a whimper.

"Lucky for us, my brother isn't here." My gaze locks with his, defiant and desperate all at once.

"Mais..." he growls softly, pulling back just slightly, but the tension crackles between us like static electricity.

We stay like that for a long, torturous minute, before his mouth is on mine—desperate. He drags me closer, lips crushing mine, water splashing up the sides of the tub as my hand fists in his curls. He tastes like cider and heat and every memory I've been trying to bury.

Why did I ever let him go? The thought plays in my head on a loop.

I climb onto his lap before I can think twice. His hands grip my ass, pulling me flush against him, and there it is. His hard, thick cock pressed right against the thin barrier of my bikini. The contact makes me gasp into his mouth, my hips rocking without permission.

He groans, low and guttural, grinding up against me so hard I feel him everywhere. My nipples ache under my bikini top, straining against the fabric, and he must feel it too because one of his hands slides up my back, fingers brushing the wet strap before palming my breast through the thin material.

I whimper, arching against him.

"Fuck, Maisy," he breathes, kissing down my throat, sucking against my skin until I'm sure there'll be marks tomorrow. "Did you wear this skimpy little bikini for me?"

"Yes," I gasp out as his other hand slides over my hip, down to my thigh, pulling me harder against him while he groans appreciatively.

The water makes everything slicker, hotter, and when his thumb teases the edge of my bikini, skimming just beneath the thin fabric, I nearly come undone.

"Sterling..." My voice breaks, half a plea, half a warning.

His mouth finds mine again, bruising and hungry, his tongue sliding against mine as his thumb dips lower, brushing where I ache most. My hips buck, chasing it. Sterling's fingers slide deep inside me, curling just right until I gasp and slap a hand over my mouth.

I can't—God, I can't let him hear how much I've wanted this. How much I ached for it.

His thumb presses against my clit, slow circles that make my thighs tremble under the water. My head tips back, eyes squeezed shut as if that will help me resist moaning.

"Let me see those beautiful eyes," he murmurs, gently peeling my hand from my mouth.

I force my eyes open, meeting his deep browns, focused only on me. The intensity there steals the little breath I had left.

"That's it," he coaxes, moving his fingers in a rhythm that makes my body arch toward him despite myself. "Let go, Mais. I know you're already so close."

And he's not wrong. Heat coils low in my core, building higher and higher, until I'm gripping his wrist under the water, not to stop him, but to anchor myself against the building storm inside me.

Every thrust of his fingers and flick of his thumb sends me reeling closer to the edge. My thighs clamp tight around his waist, my hips rolling helplessly against his hand. I bite down on a whimper, but it escapes anyway—desperate, breaking the quiet night.

Sterling groans under his breath like he feels it too. His forehead nearly touches mine, lips brushing the corner of my mouth as he growls, "Fuck, you're about to come for me, aren't you?"

"Yes," I whisper, shamelessly. My whole body is strung tight, seconds away from shattering.

And then he stops.

Just like that, the pressure vanishes. His fingers slip free, leaving me empty, trembling, and aching.

My whimper this time is broken, pleading, before I can swallow it down. "Sterling..."

He shakes his head, jaw clenched, eyes dark with want. "We can't. I promised your brother I wouldn't do this."

I want to scream at him, scratch him, beg him—anything to take away the throbbing need he just left me with. But I just stare at him, chest heaving, lips parted, undone.

He leans close enough that his breath ghosts my ear. "But I want you to know that I want to. That I still want you, in any way I can have you. In any way you'll let me."

I whimper again, softer this time, and hate myself for how much he hears it. The silence that follows is deafening, broken only by the bubbling jets and our ragged breaths. Moments later, he climbs out of the hot tub, still rock hard, and walks back into the house, leaving me out in the tub alone.

THIRTEEN

STERLING

TURNING MAISY DOWN—AGAIN—WAS the last thing I wanted to do. I can see it's still sitting heavy on her, because not only is she completely distracted during our lesson, but she's also doing a damn good job of avoiding my eyes whenever her goggles are off.

Last night we crossed a line. One I swore to Levi I wouldn't cross. The only reason I'm even teaching her how to snowboard is because Levi trusted me to keep my hands to myself.

When Maisy and I first started seeing each other years ago, it didn't take Levi long to put two and two together. Maisy doesn't know this, but before we were even officially dating, he pulled me aside and told me flat out that if I ever broke her heart, he'd kill me. That was the first time I'd ever seen Levi's protective side, and it scared me more than I expected.

When Maisy broke up with me, he was the first person to show up at my door. I thought he was there to finish me off since she'd already gutted me. Instead, he came with a six-pack of beer and planted himself on my couch. We spent the day watching the sports network without saying much of anything. When he finally stood to leave, he asked me to promise him one thing—that Maisy and I would never try again. That the furthest we'd ever go was friendship.

At the time, it was an easy promise to make. I couldn't picture a future where Maisy and I would ever get back together, let alone be friends. But now? After what happened last night? I feel like I've already broken that promise—fingers in places they shouldn't have been.

Maybe that promise is a blessing in disguise, because it'll keep me in check going forward. Being anything more than friends with Maisy—even just casual, even just messing around —feels too much like the life we had three years ago. A life Maisy didn't want.

Back then, life was damn near perfect. I had Maisy, the most amazing girlfriend, Levi, my best friend, their parents who treated me like one of their own, and I was right on the edge of going pro. Snowboarding was supposed to be my dream career —traveling the world, conquering mountains, and doing it all with Maisy at my side.

But when she ended things, I lost all of it in one shot. Not just her, but Levi and their parents, too. Even the career I wanted, because suddenly I couldn't picture it without her in it. So I left. I packed up and swore to myself I'd never let anything feel permanent again. Because permanence is just an illusion.

Maisy's sharp squeal yanks me out of the memory, and my heart slams against my ribs when I realize she's not practicing her edging like she should be—she's flying down the fucking mountain uncontrollably.

I snap into motion, tossing my board down, slamming my boots into the bindings, and tearing after her as fast as I can.

The slope is steep, trees closing in fast, and I push hard to catch her before she gets hurt, but I'm too late.

She crashes into a pine tree with a sickening thud, the impact knocking her flat onto her back.

"Fuck." The word tears out of me as I skid to a stop, rip out of my bindings, and sprint to her side. "Maisy, are you okay?"

She doesn't answer as she lies still, goggles hiding her face. Panic surges through me as I drop to my knees, peel the goggles away, and find her eyes squeezed shut, her throat working as if she's trying to swallow back pain.

"That was a hard hit," I say, my voice tight. "Can you move? Does anything hurt?"

Relief washes through me when her eyes finally crack open. She groans and tries to sit, but the sound she makes when she lifts her arm sends a shiver down my spine. She grabs her wrist and hisses.

"You're hurt." I gently take her forearm, tugging her glove off to check. Her wrist doesn't look broken, but it's already swelling. "It might just be—"

Maisy snatches her hand back before I can finish, shoving her glove on and muttering, "I'm fine."

Fine, my ass.

She unclips her boots and forces herself to stand, wobbling like she might topple at any second. I'm on my feet, instantly grabbing her elbow to steady her.

"Maisy, listen to me. You hit that tree hard. You can't just walk it off. We need to get you down to the medics and make sure everything is okay."

Her expression turns stone-cold. "Sterling, I said I'm fine."

She shoulders her board, starts climbing back up the slope, and I scoff as I trail after her. "Yeah, you keep saying that, but it's clear you're not."

She ignores me.

"Maisy, don't push me on this. If I have to call the ski patrol to drag you down the mountain, I will."

Still nothing.

"Fine," I snap. "Lesson's over."

She spins on me, eyes blazing. "I'm not some fragile little girl, okay? I've taken harder falls than this."

I hear the tremor in her voice, and the fear she's trying so hard to push down. I see the way her shoulders are tight, how her jaw works, and I realize that the fall scared her, maybe even pulled her back to that crash three years ago. And she's doing exactly what she did then—shutting down and pushing everyone out.

"Yeah," I say, climbing up to meet her glare. "I know. I was there. I watched you crash, I watched you get hurt, and I was the one that got blamed."

Her eyes blaze into mine, but she doesn't say a word.

"So let's not do that again," I press. "Let's get you checked out so none of us have to watch you fall apart. Sounds good?"

Her laugh is bitter. "Sorry my falling apart was such a pain for you, Sterling."

I growl in frustration. "It wasn't just me, Maisy. Your family, your friends—we all watched you shut us out after that accident."

"I'm not having this conversation," she snaps, spinning away from me.

"Will you ever?" My voice follows her as she comes to a stop, back still facing me. "It's been three years and you still won't have a real conversation about what happened."

"I told you, I felt like our relationship was distracting me from my career."

"Oh, you and I both know that's a load of bullshit."

She whirls back, eyes cold as ice. "Fine. You want the

truth? You were the perfect fuckbuddy, but a terrible boyfriend. I was so focused on being the perfect girlfriend that I stopped paying attention to my training. I broke up with you because if I'd been single—if I'd been focused on skiing—I wouldn't have gotten hurt."

The words make my chest ache.

"Maisy—"

"I broke up with you because—" Her voice cracks, her words cutting off as she stares at me with tears in her eyes.

She doesn't have to finish because I already know what she's going to say.

"You broke up with me because you didn't love me anymore," I whisper. "That's what you were going to say, wasn't it?"

She doesn't answer, but her silence is confirmation enough.

My chest aches as I take a few steps back, needing distance from the truth now burning between us. I reach for my walkie talkie.

"Ski patrol, come in. It's Sterling. I need medical transport."

"Copy that, Sterling. Snowmobile's on their way. Where are you?"

"West side, just where the trees start."

"Got it. Hang tight."

I clip the walkie back, avoiding her eyes as I crouch to strap into my board.

"What, you're just going to leave me here to wait for them alone?" Her voice sounds like she's seconds away from crumbling.

"No." I keep my gaze on the slope below. "I'm going to wait until they get you. Then I'm heading into town. Don't wait up."

"Don't wait up? What—are you planning to stay somewhere else tonight?" she asks, voice shaky.

I close my eyes. "No, Mais. I'll be back. I just need some... space."

The snowmobile arrives minutes later, and I stand aside while they help her on. As promised, I push off, carving down the mountain alone.

Away from Maisy. And away from the truth.

FOURTEEN

STERLING

"LOOK MAN, I'm going to have to cut you off," the bartender says, his rag pausing mid-swipe on the counter. His voice is calm, and it pisses me right the hell off.

"For what fuckin' reason?" I growl, gripping my glass like it's the only thing keeping me upright. "I'm fine."

He quirks a brow, unimpressed. "Look, I don't know how you're able to even string together more than two words right now, but if you keep this up, you'll drink yourself to death."

I scoff, the sound bitter in my throat. "Death would be a mercy."

"You always were the dramatic type," a familiar voice cuts in from behind me.

The stool next to me scrapes as someone sits down. I turn, blinking against the dim bar light, only to find Colton fuckin' Harrison sitting there—snow still melting into his messy hair, jacket damp from the storm outside.

He's one of the surfers on the Saltwater Shredders, but to me, he'll always be the kid I used to play basketball with after school, before he packed up and left town on a surfing scholarship.

Whenever he'd come back to town to visit his family, we'd catch a game together for old times' sake and he'd always drop Saltwater Springs into conversations, nudging me to consider moving there when I didn't know where the hell I belonged. By the time I made the move, he'd already left the team, but he hadn't been wrong. Gabriel, the team coach, had scooped me up into his orbit without hesitation.

Colton waves the bartender over, orders a beer, and then slouches comfortably against the bar.

"The fuck are you doing here?" I finally manage once my jaw finds its way off the floor. "Aren't you supposed to be in Hawaii with the rest of the team? Don't tell me you're re-joining the Rip Raiders."

Just over a year ago, Colton had run off from the Saltwater Shredders and joined the local surf team, the Rip Raiders. I don't know why he did that, considering how shit that team is, but he's back with the Shredders now, where he belongs.

"You couldn't pay me enough to join those rich fucks again." He snorts, lifting the bottle to his lips and taking a long drink. "Nah. Gabriel gave me the week off to come visit my parents. My sister's in town too."

I arch a brow. "Your Hollywood-loving, popstar sister?"

"The one and only. World's most beloved singer, and she'll never let you forget it." His laugh is dry, but his eyes are warm. He takes another pull of beer. "Anyway, what's got you holed up in this shit bar, talking about dying? Thought you'd be some-where hot, soaking in the break from work."

If I were sober, I'd keep my mouth shut. Not because I don't trust Colton, but because I hate spilling my problems on anyone.

Instead, I knock my knuckles against the bar and mutter,

"I've been teaching Maisy how to snowboard up at Levi's resort."

Colton stills mid-drink. "Maisy?" His brows shoot up. "Olympic Skier Maisy? As in your ex? The one who sent you running from this place?"

"Alright, first of all," I clear my throat, glaring at him, "I didn't run. I just didn't have anything worth staying for."

"Ouch."

"Oh, fuck off. Everyone knew you'd go back to the Shredders someday. You were never going to stay with this town's bozo surf team forever."

"True," he admits, tipping his bottle toward me like it's a toast. "But answer me this—why are you the one teaching her? Levi couldn't find anyone else? Seems cruel of him to pair you two up."

"I'm the only one he trusts not to make a move on his sister."

Colton pauses, studying me for a moment, then his lips twist into a smirk. "Let me guess. You made a move on his sister."

I groan, dragging a hand through my curls, frustration knotting in my chest. Even drunk, guilt for breaking Levi's trust coils tight in my gut.

"That, and she finally told me the real reason she left me," I mutter, wishing the bartender would take the hint and slide me one last drink.

Colton's expression sharpens. "Which is?"

"Well not only does she blame me for the accident, but apparently she fell out of love with me too."

"You're fucking shitting me." His bottle slams down on the counter. He swivels toward me fully, eyes blazing. "You don't actually believe that, right?"

I laugh, humorless and hollow. "Doesn't matter what I believe, Colt. It's what she believes."

"Come on. There's no way in hell Maisy actually meant that."

I frown, staring hard at him. "What do you mean?"

He leans in, voice lower. "You know Maisy. She's always used words like a weapon. She'll cut you deep just to build her wall higher. I think she said the one thing that she knew would wreck you—because if it hurt bad enough, you'd run again."

"I told you, I didn't run," I growl.

Colton tilts his head, eyes narrowing. "And yet you're here drinking the night away instead of talking this out with her, aren't you?"

The truth hits me like a slap.

I study him, wondering how the hell he's so damn good at reading people. "You should've been a therapist," I mutter, shoving a fifty onto the counter and pushing to my feet.

He barks a laugh. "I'll stick to surfing."

Outside, snowflakes swirl under the yellow glow of the streetlights. Colton shoulders my weight when I stumble, staying with me until a cab pulls up.

"I'll see you in a couple weeks, bud. Don't let me catch you back in that bar while I'm here."

"Fuck off," I mutter, sliding into the cab. His chuckle follows me, fading as the door shuts.

He's right, though. Leaving Maisy behind when the ski patrol showed up was just another way of running. I should've stayed. I should've made sure she went to the medic myself. Should've made sure she wasn't injured. Should've seen through the words she used to push me away.

But I didn't.

I was too wrapped up in how her words made *me* feel. Too

focused on *my* own pain. And maybe that's always been the problem.

By the time the cab winds up the mountain road and stops in front of the chalet, it's past midnight. I tap my card against the payment terminal, stagger out into the biting cold, and fix my blurry eyes on the front door that feels a mile away. Each step is clumsy and heavy, but I finally shove it open, only to collapse face first on the welcome mat inside.

"Sterling," Maisy gasps, bolting off the couch. She kneels beside me, eyes wide, voice panicked. "Are you okay?"

"I am now that you're here." I smirk with my eyes closed.

"You're drunk."

It's not a question.

She hooks my arm over her shoulder, kicks the door shut behind us, and half-carries me down the hall. The world sways, but she steadies me, stubborn as ever.

"I know what you did earlier," I rasp when my bedroom door comes into sight.

Her grip tightens. "What did I do?"

"You fed me some bullshit."

She glances up, brow furrowed. "What the hell are you talking about?"

A crooked smirk tugs at my lips as I fix my gaze on the door ahead. "I don't believe you blame me for the accident, and I don't believe you ever fell out of love with me. I think you did what you always do when you're scared—push me away."

She stops walking, the air between us stilling. I brace for her sharp words, the argument that always comes next, but she stays quiet.

"What, you're not going to fight me on it? Try to prove me wro—"

"You're right." The words punch the breath out of me. "I'm sorry."

"I'm starting to feel like you'll never tell me the real reason you left," I whisper moments later, finally looking down at her.

She keeps her eyes on the floor, sadness dimming the spark in them. "Maybe, maybe not. It wouldn't change anything."

"It'd give me closure, Mais." My laugh is hollow. "I'm still hung up on you because I can't stop trying to figure out what I did to lose you."

"You didn't do anything." She finally meets my gaze, her eyes glassy.

"Yeah, well...maybe that's the problem."

She exhales, the sound shaky, and starts walking again. "Let's get you to bed. This isn't a conversation for tonight."

FIFTEEN

MAISY

I WAKE up to the smell of coffee floating through the air. My lashes flutter open, and the first thing I see is the faint glow of the fireplace across the living room, embers still alive from last night.

Shit.

After helping Sterling to bed last night, I tried going to my own bed, but the silence there had been too loud, my thoughts sprinting laps in the dark, so I came back out to read on the couch and I guess I must've fallen asleep out here.

A sudden clink of ceramic behind me jolts me upright. My heart thuds before I remember where I am, and I twist slowly, peeking over the back of the couch. A few strands fall loose into my face, and I quickly tuck them behind my ear—only to freeze at what I see.

Sterling in the kitchen, bare-chested, muscles flexing as he pours steaming coffee into a mug. A towel hangs carelessly over one broad shoulder. Morning light from the windows cuts across his torso, carving shadows into every ridge of his stomach, the sharp V at his hips leading down into the waistband of low-slung sweats.

"Holy shit," I whisper before I can stop myself.

My gaze drags helplessly downward and back up again, like I've got zero control over my own eyes. He was hot three years ago, but now he's lethal. As if he feels it, his head tilts, eyes finding mine across the room. That familiar smirk curves at his lips.

"Coffee?" His voice is rough, sleep-worn, and God, it does something low in my stomach.

The glint in his eye tells me he knows exactly what I'm thinking about. He slides one of the mugs forward on the counter, a silent offering, his brow raised like he's daring me not to take it.

"Uhm—yeah," I say too quickly, pushing myself upright. The blanket that had been thrown over me tumbles to the floor. I frown at it—I don't remember covering myself. Did he...?

My cheeks burn at the thought.

I shuffle to the counter and wrap my fingers around the warm mug, grateful for something to do with my hands. Sterling pours a second cup for himself, moving easily, like he hadn't been stumbling drunk only hours ago.

"How're you feeling?" I ask, lifting the cup to my lips.

"Surprisingly...not horrible," he says, raising his own mug. Then he pauses. "But I don't remember a single damn thing."

The words make me freeze mid-sip. I set my mug down slowly. "Nothing?"

He shakes his head, rubbing the back of his neck, brows knit as he digs through the fog. "The last thing I remember is you crashing into that tree on the mountain."

I blink. That's hours before he got home drunk. Before I hurled lies at him to push him away—words I wish I could swallow back down. I stare at him, and he looks back at me innocently, but I don't know whether he's being serious or not.

"Is that normal?" I ask carefully. "That's a huge chunk of time to lose, Sterling. You were still sober when I crashed. Maybe you should get checked out at the hospital, just to be safe?"

He waves me off with a sip of coffee, like I'm overreacting. "Nah. It usually comes back after a few days. A shitty side-effect of drinking too much."

If he's being honest about not remembering, that means in a few days, he'll remember every single word I said. Bile rises in my throat.

"I...said some not-so-nice things to you," I admit, voice low. "After the crash. I know you don't remember, but I'm sorry."

His mouth tilts up, one corner lifted in that crooked almost-smile. "Don't worry about it. I'm sure it wasn't as bad as you're making it sound."

I give him a weak smile back, though the truth tastes bitter on my tongue. It was worse. Way worse.

He sets his mug down and leans on the counter. "Why don't you grab a shower while I start breakfast?"

I arch a brow. "Wow. Is that your subtle way of saying I look like shit?"

He snorts. "Maisy, you could never look like shit."

Heat prickles across my cheeks. I hide behind another sip of coffee, pretending his words don't send my stomach flipping. "You wouldn't say that if you saw me hungover."

"Ah, right." His grin spreads. "I almost forgot you drink now. We'll have to get you wasted before I leave, just so I can witness Hungover Maisy in all her glory."

"In your dreams, Sterling." I roll my eyes. "Thanks for the coffee." I slip away toward the shower, his gaze heavy on my back.

THE MOUNTAIN AIR is crisp when we get to the resort earlier than usual, the slopes mostly deserted. I've always loved mornings like this—the world still asleep, the snow untouched, the mountains rising endless around us. It feels surreal.

On the ski lift, my hands clamp around the safety bar, the cable hums above us as we glide higher, and beside me, Sterling turns just enough to watch me, his profile defined against the rising sun.

"You know what I'll never understand?" he asks, smirk tugging at his lips. "How the hell you're a pro skier but terrified of ski lifts."

"I *was* a pro skier," I correct. "Past tense."

"You're still a pro skier, Maisy," he says firmly, his voice holding something that makes every hair on my neck stand on end. "And I don't get it. You'd launch off jumps almost this high every day. But this?" He gestures to the lift, incredulous.

A laugh escapes me, one that feels foreign, but good. "It's different. Up here, I'm not in control. The cord could snap, and there's nothing I can do. We'd just...fall."

"And what about your ski tricks?"

"At least with those, if I saw the fall coming, I could adjust. Maybe not save it completely, but soften the blow."

He hums, quiet for a beat. "So it's about control."

I nod.

His gaze lingers on me. "Is that what you did, that year of your injury? Adjusted for the fall?"

Memories slam into me—the jump that felt all too wrong, the crowd's gasp, the sickening impact. I swallow hard, then nod. "Yeah. Instead of snapping my neck in front of everyone, I shifted enough to only cause a herniated disc."

He goes silent, staring out at the mountains. I can't read his expression. Finally, he looks back at me and murmurs, "I'm sorry. I shouldn't have left."

A bitter laugh slips out before I can stop it. "I basically forced you out. And anyway—it doesn't matter. It's in the past."

He doesn't argue, but he doesn't look away, either. His silence says more than words ever could. By the time we reach the practice zone, the air between us is heavy.

"Alright," he says, shifting into instructor mode. "Yesterday proved we've got to keep working on your edging, unless you want to risk another out-of-control ride and a repeat of your tragic assault on that poor tree."

"Hey!" I smack his arm, laughing despite myself. His grin is wicked, teasing, and it pulls one out of me too.

"Let's start with something called the Falling Leaf."

"What the hell is that?"

"Think of how a leaf drifts down in a zigzagging motion, back and forth. That's what you'll do. Sideslip your board in controlled zigzags all the way down." He tosses his board onto the snow, clips in, and winks at me. "It'll give you complete control."

I clip into my board, raising a brow. "I doubt it'll be as easy as you're making it sound."

"You never liked easy anyway," he fires back, smirking as he pushes off.

SIXTEEN

STERLING

TWO WEEKS of teaching Maisy how to snowboard has reminded me of something I'd almost forgotten—she's an adrenaline junkie, through and through. The girl lives for the rush.

Two weeks ago, she was clumsy, stiff on the board, cursing under her breath every time she caught an edge. But now? She's practically carving down the mountain like she's been doing it for years. Every run gets smoother, and she doesn't even hesitate at the steeper pitches. Watching her ride, I get flashes of the Maisy I used to know—the one who'd launch herself off insane ski jumps with zero fear and laugh the whole way down.

And damn if it isn't amazing to witness.

We stop halfway down the slope, collapsing into the snow with our boards unstrapped, breath puffing into the cold morning air. She tips her head back to drink from her water bottle, cheeks pink from the wind, dark hair tumbling out from under her helmet.

"Why'd you give up snowboarding?" she asks, wiping her

mouth with the back of her glove. "I really thought you were gonna pursue it professionally."

My gaze drops, drawn to the town of Bluewater Bluffs stretched out at the base of the mountain. The view should be peaceful, grounding. Instead, it makes my chest tight.

How do I explain it without it sounding like I'm blaming her? Because the truth is messy.

"I think I realized my idea of what that career would look like wasn't going to happen the way I pictured it," I say carefully. "And once I accepted that, I didn't want it anymore."

Maisy goes quiet, following my gaze down to the town. "Because I wouldn't be there with you?"

I don't answer, keeping my eyes locked on the view like it's suddenly the most interesting thing in the world. If I open my mouth, I'll either say too much or not enough. And I can't risk either.

I've realized she's more fragile than she lets on. She masks it well with her jokes and that sharp tongue, but I see it—the doubt in her eyes, the heaviness she carries. It's why I gave her an out for the things she said to me two weeks ago after her crash. Words that cut deep. Words I still hear at night when everything's quiet.

She's asked me more than once if I remember, and I keep pretending that I don't. It's easier that way. She doesn't need to live with the guilt of knowing I do. I'll carry it for both of us until she forgets she ever said those words.

"Do you ever regret it?" she asks, voice barely above a whisper.

My gaze drops to my boots, snow dusting the tips. My brows pull together. "Sometimes."

The word tastes strange out loud, like admitting a secret I've kept buried too long. There are days I wish I'd stuck with it

—just to prove I could do it. To myself, to everyone. Even if I'd been doing it alone. *Especially* if I'd been doing it alone.

Maisy nudges me with her shoulder, snapping me out of my head. "So why don't you try getting back into it?"

I look over and she's smiling a small, genuine smile. It makes my chest ache in a way I don't want to admit. Unlike her, I still have the option. I could chase it again, if I wanted. But I don't, because somewhere deep down, I think I've been punishing myself by staying away. Because a part of me really does believe I'm to blame for what happened to her—for her fall, for her injury, for all the things she lost because of it.

And maybe if I give up the thing I love, it balances the scales.

"I don't know, Mais," I finally say, my voice rough. "I've got a whole new life in Saltwater Springs shaping boards for the surf team. That's where I fit now. And even if I wanted to, I'm so out of practice I don't think I could compete at that level. Not anymore, and especially not at my age."

Her head snaps toward me, eyes wide. "You're not even thirty yet," she scoffs, like I've said the dumbest thing imaginable.

I huff out a laugh, rolling my shoulders. "Yeah, well, try telling that to my back." My joints pop in protest as I push to my feet and strap into my board again. The movement feels mechanical, something my body remembers even if it doesn't move as fluidly as it used to. I turn toward her, raising a brow. "Race you to the bottom?"

Maisy's eyes light up instantly with a fire that I've always loved seeing, fierce and uncontained. She jumps to her feet and fumbles with her bindings, strapping in quickly. "You're on, loser."

Before I can even count down, she's already flying forward, a blur of motion and laughter.

"Hey!" I shout, laughing as I push off to follow her.

Even though I could easily pass her, cut close and leave her trailing behind, I don't. Because her laughter carried back on the wind does something to me I can't begin to explain. Seeing her take back a piece of herself on this mountain is worth more than any win.

So I let her take it.

By the time we come to a stop at the base of the slope, she's doubled over, laughing and breathless. I roll up behind her, snow spraying as I brake.

"Damn," she says between gulps of air, "you really are out of practice. You're lucky I can't compete anymore because I dusted your ass."

I roll my eyes, trying—and failing—to smother my grin. "Ha-ha. Very funny."

Her smirk grows cocky, the kind of expression that used to drive me insane back when we were kids racing each other down every hill we could find—her on skis and me on a board.

"Oh, come on, Sterling," she says, her voice dipping into flirty teasing as she unclips from her board. "Don't be a sore loser. What's my prize for winning?"

I don't even think before I move. My hand shoots forward, catching the front of her neck gaiter, and I tug her toward me. She gasps, her boots scraping against the snow as she stumbles forward. Instinctively, her hands splay across my chest to steady herself, and I feel the heat of her through the layers. For a second, neither of us breathes.

Her wide eyes lock on mine, then drop downward, lingering on my mouth before darting back up. My lips twitch into a smirk.

"What would you like your prize to be, Hart?" My voice drops lower than I intend.

Her breath catches, visible in the cold, and the corner of her mouth curves. "I think you know what I want."

Every muscle in my body tightens and I feel my cock already starting to come to life. My eyes drop to her lips, hungry and aching, the need to close the distance almost unbearable. But the thought of Levi—of the promise I made him—shoves its way in between us.

"You really don't give a shit that I promised your brother I wouldn't cross that line, huh?" I murmur, though my restraint is paper thin.

Maisy's eyes darken with defiance, her voice steady even as her fingers curl tighter into my jacket. "I really don't. My brother doesn't get to make those decisions for me. It's my boundary to set." She leans in, close enough that I feel the brush of her breath against my mouth.

Her lips are right there, so damn close I can almost taste her—

"Maisy!"

We both jerk apart as Levi's voice cuts through the air, dragging my attention up the slope. He's a few yards away, board propped casually under his arm, though the frown on his face tells me he's been watching long enough.

Maisy stiffens beside me, her hands slipping from my chest, and my grip on her neck gaiter lingers a second longer than it should before I finally let go.

"Everything good down here?" Levi calls, suspicion clear in the bite of his tone.

Maisy clears her throat, pasting on a smile that doesn't reach her eyes. "Yeah, we were just racing. And I won."

Levi's gaze narrows, lingering on me like he knows exactly how close I was to giving in.

I force a smirk, even though my blood is still roaring with

the taste of almost. "And your sister dusted me. Guess I'm out of practice."

Levi's mouth ticks into something that's not quite a smile, not quite a scowl. He nods once, slow, eyes lingering on me a beat too long before he finally looks back to his sister.

"Try not to kill each other on my mountain," he says, before turning his board into the snow like that's all he came for.

Maisy waits until his back is fully turned, then tilts her face toward me. Her lips curl into a reckless and knowing grin, like she's daring me to care that Levi almost caught us. Her eyes glimmer, holding mine for a second before she returns to her board with a huff, like nothing happened.

But something *did* happen. And it's only getting harder to ignore.

SEVENTEEN

MAISY

I'M CURLED up on the couch across from Sterling, a paperback open in my hands, pretending to read while he's absorbed in whatever he's doing on his laptop. The words on the page blur together, meaningless, because all I can think about is what happened earlier.

The almost kiss.

If Levi hadn't interrupted us on the slope, what would've happened? Would Sterling have actually kissed me? The look in his eyes had said yes, and I don't blame him. I wanted it even more than he did. I *still* want it.

Sterling cooked dinner when we got home—steak and mashed potatoes—and instead of disappearing into his bedroom, he parked himself on the couch with his laptop.

I contemplate whether I should start the conversation and confront the elephant in the room. Stealing another glance, I notice how his jaw is sharply defined in the glow of the screen, brows furrowed in concentration. He looks up, catching me staring, and I nearly drop my book to the floor. My eyes dart back down to the page, flipping it without a clue of what the hell I just read.

After a few minutes, I peek back up at him and he's returned to focusing on his laptop, but there's an amused glimmer in his eyes.

Great. He totally knows I'm staring again.

I clear my throat, forcing myself to focus. This time, I swear I'm actually going to read, but before I can make it two sentences in, the room plunges into darkness, and the soft hum of appliances dies. The only light left is Sterling's laptop glow.

"What the hell?" I mutter, already digging my phone from the cushions to tap on the flashlight. A weak beam shines across the room.

Sterling closes his laptop and turns on his flashlight too. "Do we need to flip the breaker?"

I pad to the west-side window, pressing close to the glass. Down in Bluewater Bluffs, the town lights blink off in waves, a domino trail until the whole valley is swallowed in shadow. "I don't think flipping the breaker is going to help. It's not just us —it's everywhere."

"Town-wide blackout?" He comes to stand beside me, shoulder brushing mine as we both look out.

"Looks like it."

He exhales, running his hand through his hair before heading toward the back door. "Then I'd better get the fire going. Don't want us freezing to death if this lasts."

I watch as he disappears onto the back deck, his flashlight beam bobbing while he grabs a couple of logs from the wood-pile. He returns with them balanced easily under one arm, the other tugging the door shut with a thud.

He kneels at the fireplace, sleeves shoved up past his elbows, and my eyes betray me—fixating on him instead of what he's doing.

His forearms are all lean strength, sinew shifting beneath tanned skin. Veins ridge the surface, not in an overdone way, but enough to remind me how easily those hands could pin me, hold me, protect me. When he presses the newspaper into the grate, the muscles in his wrist flex, a smooth ripple that makes my stomach tighten.

The lighter sparks, flames catching fast, the crackle of burning paper filling the silence before the logs flare.

"Thanks," I murmur.

The warmth licks at my skin as the glow stretches into the room, but I'm not watching the fire at all. I'm watching him. Watching the way strength looks effortless on him, the way his body feels like a memory. And God help me, I can't stop wondering how those arms would feel if they wrapped around me again.

I sink back into the couch and raise my book like a shield, trying to keep his arms from view before he notices, but Sterling crosses the room, plucks the book straight from my hands, and sets the bookmark in before he closes it with a firm snap.

"Hey!" I reach for it, frowning.

"If I don't get to be productive," he says, smirking down at me, "you don't get to hide in your book."

"Uh, excuse me?" I protest. "I wasn't hiding. Plus, I never told you that you couldn't go back on your laptop."

He sighs, tapping a knuckle lightly against my head like he's testing for hollowness. "Power's out, genius. That means no Wi-Fi."

Heat rushes to my face. "Oh, right."

He smirks harder at my embarrassment, shoving his hands into his pockets. "So, what do we do now?"

I shrug, fighting the flutter in my chest. "You tell me."

Sterling thinks for a beat, the fire painting shadows across his features. "Do you have any board games?"

A smile spreads across my face. "Actually...yes."

I hop up, my excitement tugging me across the room to the bookshelf. Kneeling, I rummage through the bottom shelf until my hand lands on the box I've been looking for. I turn back to him with a grin.

He ambles over, slowly, like he knows I'm watching the way his body moves. My heart kicks up a notch in response because how can he have changed so much in just three years?

When he sees what I'm holding, his brows shoot up. "Candyland?"

"The original version," I say proudly.

He takes the box, studying it like it's some ancient relic. "Is there a difference between this one and the newer one?"

I take the box back from him and plop onto the rug in front of the fire, the game in my lap. "The art is better. The new one looks cheap."

His chuckle rumbles low, and when I glance up, his eyes are still on me, the firelight flickering across them in a way that makes my stomach flip.

Focus, Maisy.

Sterling disappears into the kitchen while I set up the board on the rug, smoothing it flat. A moment later, I hear the pop of a cork, and when I look over, he's walking back with a bottle of red in one hand and two glasses dangling from the other.

My brows shoot up. "What, we're turning Candyland into a drinking game now?"

He smirks, setting the bottle on the side table beside us before lowering himself to the floor next to me. "Why not? High stakes. Loser drinks."

"Pretty sure that's not how Candyland was designed," I tease, watching him pour a glass and hand it to me. His fingers brush mine when I take it, lingering a second too long and causing my pulse to stutter.

He shrugs, pouring his own. "Then consider this the adult edition."

I sip the smooth wine, warming me from the inside out. "You realize you're going to regret this when you're chugging glass after glass, right?"

Sterling chuckles low in his throat, leaning back on one arm, wine glass in the other. "Confidence looks dangerously good on you." He raises his glass in a mock toast, eyes holding mine. "To dangerous confidence."

I clink my glass against his, my heart racing. "And to your impending defeat."

He grins, that slow, devastating grin that always undoes me, and sets his glass down beside the board.

"Let's play."

Sterling fans out the cards between his big hands, shaking them like he's shuffling for high stakes poker instead of a kid's game.

"Alright, rules are simple," he says, a playful challenge in his eyes. "Every time you hit a setback—stuck square, licorice, whatever it's called—you drink."

I snort, tucking my legs under me as I settle closer to the fire. "Whatever."

His smirk tilts. "You're not backing down, are you?"

I meet his gaze head-on and lift my glass. "Not a chance."

When we start, Sterling picks the blue game piece, and I pick the red. He pulls the first card, moves his piece, and smirks up at me like he's already winning. I roll my eyes and take my turn.

When I land on a licorice square, Sterling leans toward me, my glass in his hand, and murmurs, "Drink up, Hart," as he passes it to me.

I groan, taking a dramatic sip before narrowing my eyes at

him. "Enjoy this moment, because it's the last one you're getting."

"Big talk," he teases, his knee bumping mine as he slides his pawn across the board. The touch should be casual, but he doesn't move it, and neither do I.

The wine loosens us both while we play, and by the time I pull a card that rockets me ahead, I can't help squealing with excitement. "Oh my God, yes!"

Sterling leans back on his hands, watching me with that slow grin. "Look at you. Smug as hell. I should make you drink for celebrating too hard."

"Not in the rules," I sing-song, taking a sip anyway, just to taunt him.

"I don't remember making a rule that prevents adding rules while playing," he says, eyes sliding down to my mouth before dragging back up.

I feel it like a spark under my skin, and my pulse skips. To cover it, I stick my tongue out at him and nudge his shoulder. "You're just mad I'm winning."

He leans in so close that the warmth of the fire, the wine, and his presence all blur together. "Maybe I'm letting you win, like I did on the slope."

"I won fair and square," I protest.

"Of course you did," he says, with a lazy smirk.

His hand brushes mine when he goes for his glass, fingers grazing just enough to make my breath catch. I lift my own glass and sip to distract myself, but the glass trembles slightly in my grip.

"Careful, Mais," he mumbles, watching me over the rim of his glass. "You're gonna spill."

"I'm fine," I say quickly, but my voice betrays me, soft and shaky.

He doesn't call me out, his smirk lingering as he flips his

next card and slides his pawn forward, like he's playing two games at once—Candyland, and me.

And he's winning both.

I move my pawn along the path, trying not to look too smug when I land on a shortcut. Sterling groans, dragging a hand through his hair like the fate of the world depends on Candyland.

"You're cheating somehow," he mutters.

I grin, sipping the last of my wine. "You can't cheat in Candyland, *genius*. It's pure luck."

"Or witchcraft," he says, narrowing his eyes at me in mock suspicion.

I laugh, but the sound hitches as a shiver runs through me. Damn. That happens every time I drink because my body loves to overreact, even when I'm not cold.

Sterling notices instantly, and his head tilts, brows furrowing. "You're cold."

"I'm not, I swear—"

But before I can explain, he's already reaching behind him, snagging the thick knit blanket off of the couch. He unfolds it and then, without a second's hesitation, tugs me straight into his side.

My heart kicks up. "Sterling—"

"Shut up and let me help for once," he murmurs, pulling the blanket around both of us until I'm cocooned against him. His chest is firm beneath my cheek, radiating warmth, his arm heavy and protective across my shoulder.

I should move and laugh it off, push him away, something. *Anything*. But instead, I breathe him in—soap and amber and something distinctly *him*—and melt into the solid line of his body. This is exactly where I want to be.

"Better?" he asks, voice low near my temple.

I nod, though the shivering hasn't stopped. It's not the cold.

It's the wine, the fire, the way every nerve ending in my body is suddenly on high alert because he's holding me like this. It's the adrenaline of being near Sterling.

The game sits abandoned on the rug, our pieces stranded mid-board. His thumb strokes idly against my arm through the blanket, sending tiny sparks shooting under my skin.

I miss this. It feels so right to be in his arms like this, like a piece of me that's been missing for the last three years is finally back, completing me. I tip my head back without meaning to, and when I do, I find his eyes already on me.

The world narrows to the steady beat of my heart in my ears, the firelight reflected in his gaze, and the way his lips part just slightly as if he's contemplating something.

He doesn't move for a long, breathless second. Then, slowly, like he's giving me every chance to pull away, he lowers his mouth to mine.

The kiss is soft at first, but the second my lips part, he deepens it. His hand slides up, cupping my jaw, angling me toward him, and I sigh into him like I've been holding my breath for weeks.

The blanket slips off my shoulder as I twist closer, clutching his shirt in my fist. His lips are warm, insistent, stealing every thought from my head until there's nothing but heat and want and the rush of finally, *finally* letting go.

The hand that's not cradling my jaw slides down, gripping my hip through the blanket, tugging me closer until I'm straddling him.

A soft sound escapes from me, half gasp, half moan, and his lips press harder, hungrier. His tongue teases mine, and I can taste the wine—sweet and dizzying. My fingers tug at his shirt, desperate to be closer.

"Fuck, Maisy," Sterling groans into my mouth, the sound

vibrating straight through me, and it makes me burn everywhere at once.

His hand skims down my thigh, squeezing, before sliding back up under the blanket. My skin tingles in its wake, heat pooling low in my stomach. I tilt my head, opening for him, and the kiss turns needy—messy, devouring, like we can't get enough of each other. My body hums with it, alive in a way I haven't felt in forever.

But just as quickly, the lamp on the side table blazes to life, the hum of the fridge roars from the kitchen, and the overhead lights flood the room in sudden brightness.

Sterling freezes and so do I when we realize the power's back. Our lips hover just barely apart, breaths colliding, both of us wide-eyed in the shock of being caught by reality itself.

Sterling blinks first, swallowing hard as he leans back slightly. "The power's back."

I bite my lip, heart racing, still clutching his shirt like I'm not ready to let go. Slowly, I loosen my grip and climb off him, trying to catch my breath, pretending like my whole world didn't just tilt on its axis.

"I think I should go to bed," I whisper, breathless.

He doesn't argue. He just nods, slow and deliberate. "Yeah." Rising to his feet, he offers me his hand. "That's probably a good idea."

I slip my fingers into his, letting him pull me up—but instead of releasing me, his thumb brushes once across my knuckles before he exhales. "I'm sorry," he murmurs. "I shouldn't have—"

I cut him off before he finishes. "Don't," I say firmly, meeting his eyes. "Not a single thing that happened tonight needs an apology."

Surprise flickers in his gaze, and I squeeze his hand once before letting go. "Goodnight. I'll see you in the morning."

His jaw tightens, like there's more he wants to say, but all that comes out is a quiet, "Good night."

I walk to my room, leaving the board game on the floor and Sterling standing in the living room as he watches me go.

Behind the safety of my door, my back hits the wood and I press my palms to my face, willing my breath to even out. Because the awful, brutal truth is that I want him. I want Sterling like a starving person wants food, like no time has passed, like I didn't ruin everything we were.

And that's the part that guts me. How can I even want him, when I'm the reason he left in the first place? When I'm the one who broke us, who pushed him away, who couldn't stand to let him see me shattered and weak?

I thought I was protecting him. Instead, I destroyed him.

And now he's here again.

And wanting him feels like reaching for something I already lost.

Something I don't deserve.

EIGHTEEN

MAISY

STERLING PULLS my truck into the parking lot of the outdoor skating rink in town. I stay quiet as I stare out the window at the strings of lights twinkling above the ice and the couples gliding hand in hand, cheeks pink, and scarves fluttering while they laugh.

It's *Couples Night*, and the irony of being here with Sterling isn't lost on me.

We haven't talked about what happened between us the other night during the blackout, but it's been replaying in my mind like a broken record. The feel of his mouth, his hands, the need that nearly consumed me whole. It's becoming painfully unbearable just being around him after that.

"Remind me again why we agreed to this?" I mutter as I watch a couple on the ice spin in each other's arms like they're rehearsing a figure skating routine.

"Because your brother asked us to wingman for him tonight," Sterling replies calmly, watching the same couple.

Levi called bright and early yesterday morning to check if Sterling and I had survived the blackout, and before hanging up, he casually begged us to team up and wingman him on a date with—as he put it—*"the hottest girl on the planet."*

I blow out a frustrated breath. "Of all the places Levi could've picked for a fake double date, he had to pick the rink?" I push the door open, my boots sinking into the snow as I hop out.

Sterling rounds the car, meeting me at the back with a lazy grin. "Remind me again why you hate skating?"

I shake my head quickly. "The idea of falling flat on rock hard ice sounds like a terrible plan. Especially after the accident."

"Don't worry," he says, taking my hand in his as we start walking to the skate rental booth. "I'll make sure you don't fall."

I look down at our joined hands, basking in the warmth, and then back up at him. "What are you doing?"

"Pretty sure this is called holding hands, Maisy," he deadpans.

"I can see that," I shoot back. "But why?"

He lifts my hand to his mouth and presses a slow kiss to the back of it, causing my entire body to burn up, like there's a fire racing under my skin.

"Because we're supposed to be pretending that we're here for a double date with your brother and some girl," he says, that smirk tugging at the corner of his mouth like he knows exactly what he's doing to me.

"Okay," I breathe, trying not to let my knees buckle. "But shouldn't you save that for when they're actually watching?"

He stops us in the middle of the lot, his hand leaving mine and sliding up the side of my neck, pulling me closer until his forehead rests against mine. His breath ghosts over my lips, not quite a kiss, but so damn close my body screams for it.

"Your heart's beating so fast," he whispers, eyes closed, a

smile grazing his lips as his thumb gently strokes the side of my neck where my pulse is pounding.

Heat flares up my neck, blooming into my cheeks, and words clog my throat.

His voice dips lower. "Your brother's going to kick my ass for getting this close to you, but I'm starting to not care."

The spell breaks when Sterling finally pulls back, his gaze moving beyond me. I turn, finding Levi standing stiff near the skate rental booth with a blonde woman straight out of a ski-bunny calendar—designer cropped jacket, blown-out hair, and lips that look freshly injected. Levi's hands are balled into fists, and the way his eyes shift between me and Sterling makes my stomach drop.

"How long has he been standing there?" I murmur.

"I noticed him around when I got out of the car," Sterling says casually, his palm reclaiming mine.

Levi's gaze drops pointedly to our hands as we walk up, tension crackling in the air.

"Sorry we're late," I say quickly, hoping to smooth things over. "I had to wait for the shower water to heat up after Sterling's hour-long shower."

Levi doesn't answer, still locked in some silent battle of wills with Sterling. I turn to the blonde, desperate for relief, but instead of helping, she's staring at Sterling like he's her dessert. My stomach sours instantly. She's supposed to be on a date with my brother, not drooling over mine.

Before I can think better of it, I drop Sterling's hand and wrap my arms around his waist instead. His arm circles me without hesitation, pulling me tight against his side, and I lean into him deliberately.

The blonde's eyes cut to me, narrowing as if she's been caught. She clutches Levi's arm with nails sharp enough to draw blood.

"Babe," she whines in a singsong Australian accent. "You haven't introduced me."

Levi clears his throat, shooting me a stern look when he realizes I've wrapped myself around Sterling.

"Right. This is my sister, Maisy," he says, waving in my direction. "Maisy, this is..."

His eyes go round, and I realize he's forgotten her name. Typical Levi.

"Bri—"

Her head whips in his direction, eyes narrowed. It's definitely not whatever the hell he was just about to say. He clears his throat and puts on his most flirtatious grin before wrapping an arm around her waist and pulling her into his side.

"*This* is my beautiful date."

Wow. Somehow, that actually works and she melts into him. I roll my eyes, slowly stepping out of Sterling's hold and straightening when he offers his hand out to her.

"I'm Sterling," he says as she wraps her talons around his hand, giving him a suggestive smile. "I don't think I caught your name."

"Oh." She giggles, her gaze still sticky on him. "I'm Courtney."

Levi shoots Sterling a thankful look, like he didn't just look ready to murder him a minute ago.

We make our way over to the skate rental booth, each of us getting a pair before heading to the benches outside the rink. Everyone laces up quickly except me, my fingers fumbling.

"Jeez, Maisy," Levi groans. "You're slower than the five-year-olds here."

I look up and glare at him, biting my tongue so I don't embarrass him in front of Courtney. Not that it matters because she's back to ogling Sterling right in front of me.

"You know I hate skating," I mutter.

He rolls his eyes. "Grow up."

Before I can explode, Sterling steps between us. "How about you and Courtney hit the ice first," Sterling suggests. "I'll help get Maisy's skates on."

Levi doesn't think twice as he takes hold of Courtney's hand and drags her onto the ice. I watch as they effortlessly skate off just like everybody else on the rink, and I feel anxiety building in my chest.

"I don't think I can do this," I whisper.

"Yes, you can." Sterling crouches in front of me, steady hands on my ankle as he props my skate on his thigh and tightens the laces for me. His head is bent, but his voice is low and sure. "You're the bravest person I know, Mais."

"I could get hurt," I whisper.

He pauses, tying off the lace before moving to the other foot. "I won't let that happen."

"But what if—"

"Maisy." His tone turns sharp as he tugs the lace firmly. His eyes flick up, steadily. "If you fall, then you land on me. I won't let you get hurt."

The conviction in his voice makes my chest ache.

"Okay," I whisper.

Sterling pulls me up, holding both my hands as we step toward the rink. The cold air nips my cheeks, the sound of blades scraping the ice filling my ears. He guides me as we make our way onto the ice, skating backward while I cling to his forearms, stiff and shaky like a newborn deer.

He steers us away from the edge, closer to the middle of the rink where couples and children glide slow and easy. "Ready to finally skate?"

"I'm ready for this date to be over," I mutter.

He glides closer to me now, our chests almost touching as I grip onto him. "Aw come on," he says in a low, teasing voice. "You used to love our dates. *Especially* the happy endings."

I let out a slow, measured breath as I hold his gaze. The ache between my thighs already feels torturous as I remember us getting lost in each other's bodies after every date all those years ago.

"Are we going to talk about it?" I finally ask.

His brows lift. "Talk about what?"

I force myself to look away, eyes catching on Courtney giggling as Levi shows off some spin. My throat tightens. "About what happened...during Candyland."

His hand slides under my chin, tilting my face back to him. His eyes hold mine with intensity. "Do you *want* to talk about it?"

My eyes dip down, but a small nudge of his hand has them focusing back on Sterling's face. "I don't know," I admit, voice cracking. "I kinda feel like we should."

Sterling nods, but something catches his attention behind me. I turn to look and find Levi and Courtney skating toward us now.

"Talk about it on the drive home?" he suggests quietly.

I nod just as they reach us.

"Look at you," Levi says, half surprised, half impressed. "Didn't think you'd make it past the railing, sis."

Courtney giggles, twirling her blonde hair around a manicured finger. "She's lucky to have such a strong boyfriend," she purrs, her eyes darting to Sterling like she's testing how far she can push me.

My jaw tightens, and before I can stop myself, I press closer into him, and he responds instantly, sliding an arm around my waist to steady me, but the pressure of his hand against my hip feels anything but casual.

"Oh they're not—" Levi stops himself remembering that he

asked Sterling and I to fake date for this. "She *is* lucky, isn't she?" he says instead, before pulling Courtney off to the side again to show off some more.

Sterling dips his head slightly, his breath brushing over the shell of my ear. "Relax," he murmurs, only for me to hear. "Eyes on me, Mais. Not them."

My chest squeezes, and I realize it's not just the skating making my pulse go haywire—it's him. Always him.

After a few more show-off tricks, Levi swoops in, takes Courtney's hand, and skates them both toward the far end of the rink. I track them with my eyes, frowning when they keep going, ducking past the gate that leads off the ice where they remove their skates in a hurry before rushing into the woods beside the rink.

Sterling notices too. "Are they seriously—"

"Yep," I cut in, my lip curling in disgust. "Heading off to do God knows what in the trees like a pair of teenagers."

Sterling shakes his head, amused. "Guess it's just us then."

"Guess so."

He takes both my hands in his, skating backwards with effortless ease. "Come on, Mais. Let's do a lap."

My knees lock in protest. "Sterling—"

"Relax. I've got you." His sure tone makes me want to believe him even when I know I'm seconds from disaster.

We glide past couples holding hands and kids darting between legs, the air thick with the scent of hot chocolate and woodsmoke. For half a second, I almost feel like I'm actually enjoying skating, and then a blur of puffy jackets rockets past us. Two kids racing each other, weaving dangerously close. One cuts right behind Sterling, who's still skating backward, and panic shoots through me as my balance wobbles.

"Sterling!"

He moves faster than I thought possible, spinning us so his

body takes the fall. We crash onto the ice, but instead of pain, I land squarely on top of him, his arms tight around me.

"Told you I wouldn't let you get hurt," he groans moments later, wincing with a crooked grin.

My breath catches. My palms are splayed against his chest, his heartbeat hammering under my hands, and his face is so close—close enough that one wrong move and I'd be kissing him again.

And I want to. *God*, I want to.

But I just swallow, my cheeks flaming as I scramble off of him and onto my knees. "Are you okay?"

He chuckles, breath fogging in the night air as he sits up. "I'll be fine." He rubs the back of his head as he looks around. "If I know Levi, I don't think he's going to come back. Want to get out of here?"

I let out a relieved sigh. "I thought you'd never ask."

NINETEEN

STERLING

THE CAR RIDE UP the mountain to the chalet is heavy with silence. The wipers drag across the windshield in a steady rhythm, pushing snowflakes aside as the road winds higher. Beside me, Maisy sits angled toward the window, her breath fogging the glass. Her fingers twist anxiously in her lap, tugging at each other. I can tell her mind is racing a million miles per minute, probably replaying last night the same way I am.

"We should talk about it," I say finally, keeping my eyes on the snowy road. "The kiss."

"It was more than just a kiss, Sterling," she says, turning to look at me. "We crossed a line that exes shouldn't cross."

I hum in response, neither agreeing or denying, because the truth is I'd cross every damn line if Maisy was the one waiting for me on the other side.

A lookout point appears through the falling snow, the guardrails frosted, the wide pull-off deserted for once. Usually, it's crowded with people taking pictures of the view, but tonight it's empty. I ease the truck to the side, kill the engine, and the silence deepens until all I hear is the tick of cooling metal and the muted roar of the wind.

I turn toward her fully. "Well," I say, steadying my voice, "I don't regret crossing that line. Do you?"

Maisy doesn't answer right away. Her hands are still moving on her lap, nervous little fidgets, until she forces them flat against her thighs. She takes a deep breath, her lashes lowering as if the confession is easier to make when she isn't looking at me.

"I don't know." Her voice trembles. "Maybe I just needed to get you out of my system."

Her words sting and I try to hold my expression steady, but inside, everything twists. Get me out of her system? I've spent three years trying exactly that—changing my career, my friends, my home, my everything—but no matter what I do, she's the constant that remains. Always her.

I nod slowly, my jaw tight. "And did you? Get me out of your system?"

She turns back to the window, the snow falling thick and heavy behind the glass. For a long moment she doesn't say anything, and I let the silence stretch until I can't take it.

"Maisy?"

Her shoulders lift with a shaky inhale. "No," she whispers. "I didn't."

My heart kicks hard against my ribs, because maybe it's not possible for her to let go of me either. But there's only one way to know for sure.

I lean closer, my voice rough. "So what are you waiting for?"

She turns her head slowly, and when her eyes meet mine, they're darker than before, filled with need. I don't think as I pull the lever on my seat as far back as it'll go. She climbs over the console and into my lap, her body fitting against mine like it always belonged there.

I cup her face in both my hands, greedy and desperate, pulling her down to me. Our mouths crash together, and the kiss is like the one we shared the other night. A deep and hot collision of tongues and teeth that sucks the air straight from my lungs.

Her jacket rustles as she shoves it off, tossing it blindly into the back seat, never once breaking the kiss. Her hands work at mine next, tugging the zipper until it falls open.

When she grinds down against me, the friction is unbearable. My cock is already straining, rock hard, every nerve lit on fire by the feel of her moving over me. I break away, gasping against her lips.

"If you keep doing that," I grit out, "I'm going to come in my pants, Mais."

Her answering giggle drives me insane.

Before I can reach for her, she's sliding down my body, her knees hitting the mat on the floor of the truck. My breath punches out of me as she pulls at my jeans, yanking them and my boxers down in one determined pull. My cock springs free, thick and aching.

Maisy's eyes widen, lips parting. "Wow," she breathes. "Was it always this bi—"

I don't let her finish as my hand slides into her hair, guiding her mouth to me, and the second her lips wrap around my length, I nearly lose it. She takes me deep, farther than she ever managed before, her throat tightening around me. A guttural moan rips from my chest, my head falling back against the seat.

"Fuck, Maisy," I groan, looking down at her. Her big eyes are lifted up toward mine, glinting playfully as her mouth works over me. "You're so fucking sexy."

I swear I could die happy right now, because there's no

image in this world more perfect than Maisy Hart on her knees, lips stretched around my cock, making me forget the last three years ever happened.

Her lips slide along my length, her tongue working me with practiced strokes that make my vision blur. Every time she takes me deeper, I grip the edge of the seat tighter, my knuckles turning white as I try to hold myself back. The wet sounds her mouth makes fills the space, obscene and perfect, mixing with my ragged breathing and the soft hum of her little moans.

"Maisy..." My hand fists in her hair as my hips twitch up. "I'm so close. You're gonna make me lose it."

She pulls back with a slick pop, her hand stroking me in a slow twist while her swollen lips curve in a wicked little smile. "That's the point."

"Please tell me you're still on birth control," I beg, my head falling back.

"Of course I am," she says as she climbs back into my lap, her breath coming fast, her hair messy from where my fingers tangled in it. She looks wild, flushed, and I swear I've never seen anyone more beautiful in my life.

Her hands fumble at the button of her jeans, tugging them down with impatient jerks until she shoves them off one leg. My own hands are already there, greedy, sliding up her thighs, finding the damp heat waiting for me beneath the thin scrap of her panties.

"Fuck," I groan, my fingers brushing over the soaked fabric. "You're already dripping for me."

She gasps when I push the material aside, teasing her folds with the head of my cock. Her body jerks forward, desperate, and I bite back another curse.

"Sterling—please," she breathes, her voice breaking with urgency.

That single word undoes me. I guide myself to her, and

with one push, I'm sliding inside. Her pussy clenches around me instantly, hot and tight, pulling me deeper until I'm fully seated in her. My head falls back against the headrest as a guttural moan rips out of me.

Her nails dig into my shoulders as she adjusts, her mouth parting on a shaky exhale. "You feel even bigger than I remember."

I grab her hips, steadying her, grounding myself in the feel of her. "Let me help you get me out of your system," I grit out, lifting her slightly before slamming her back down.

She cries out, her head tipping back, her dark hair spilling over her milky shoulders. The sight is enough to drive me insane. I thrust up into her, hard and fast, each movement rocking the truck, the windows fogging from the heat our breaths and bodies create.

Maisy clings to me, moving in rhythm, grinding down as if she can't get enough. Her moans spill into the small space, sweet and breathless and completely fucking addictive.

I lean forward, capturing her mouth in a bruising kiss, swallowing her sounds as my hands roam her back, then her ass, dragging her tighter against me.

"Admit it," I growl against her lips. "Admit you still want me."

"I want you," she gasps, her forehead pressing to mine. "I never stopped wanting you."

The confession detonates inside me. I flip us, pressing her back into the seat now as I pound into her, deeper, harder, chasing the edge we're both dangling on. The truck rocks with the force of it, snow drifting heavier outside, but in here it's nothing but heat and desperation and the kind of hunger that can't be faked.

Her nails scrape down my back, her cries breaking into

moans that push me closer to the edge. I slide a hand between us, my thumb finding her clit, circling, teasing, until her whole body seizes.

"Sterling," she gasps. "Oh my God—"

She shatters around me, her body tightening, clenching, pulling me under with her. I slam into her once more, twice, before I lose it completely, groaning her name as I spill into her, the pleasure ripping through me so hard it's almost painful.

For a moment, everything goes quiet except for our panting breaths, the world narrowing down to the two of us tangled together.

Her body sags beneath me, her chest rising and falling, her lips swollen and parted. I kiss her softly this time, a contrast to the wildness of before, unable to stop myself from lingering on her mouth.

"Maisy..." I murmur, brushing my thumb along her jaw. "Tell me this wasn't just to get me out of your system."

Her lashes flutter, her gaze meeting mine, still hazy from what we just did. She swallows hard before whispering, "Maybe...maybe it can just be this. You and me, no strings. We both get what we want without complicating it."

Her words land like a punch to the ribs. Friends with benefits. That's all she's offering.

Every part of me screams that it's not enough, that I'll always want more when it comes to her, but I also know I can't walk away.

I force a small nod, my throat tight. "If that's what you want."

She gives a faint, uncertain smile, like she's trying to convince herself as much as me. "It is. You're leaving at the end of the season anyway, right?"

"Right." I lean in and kiss her again, because I'll take her however she'll let me, even if it leaves a hollow ache in my chest that I know won't fade.

And as she rests her head against mine, catching her breath, I already know the truth: I'll agree to her terms, but it won't stop me from wanting more.

TWENTY

MAISY

"I WANT YOU TO MYSELF," Sterling growls, his voice rough, breath scorching against my throat as his hips drive forward, filling me in a rhythm that makes my whole body tremble. "All mine."

He sits back on his calves without pulling out, one hand gripping my hip as his other smooths down my stomach. His gaze drops, and he watches himself slide in and out of my pussy, completely transfixed, like he's hypnotized by the way I take him.

I let myself drink in every detail of him, and God—he's beautiful. The sharp cut of his jaw is clenched in concentration, sweat beading along his brow and trickling down his temples. His chest heaves, muscles straining, every ridge of his abs shining with a sheen of sweat that makes him look carved from stone. My eyes trail lower, over the deep lines of his V, down to where his body joins mine, and my pulse skips wildly.

A moan slips from me, helpless, and I arch my back to draw him even deeper.

"Sterling..." His name tumbles from my lips on a needy sigh.

He thrusts harder, jaw locking like he's barely holding himself together. "Maisy," he grits out, voice strangled.

"Maisy."

"Yes," I gasp, nails digging into his arms. "Yes?"

"Maisy, wake up."

My eyes snap open, and the fog of my dream fades. The heat of Sterling's body is gone, along with the pressure and pleasure. Instead, I'm sprawled across the couch in the dim light of the living room, my book lying open on my chest. And Sterling—real Sterling—stands over me with a glass of water in his hands. Shirtless.

His bare skin gleams faintly in the light, those same muscles I'd just been dreaming about on full display. My cheeks burn hot.

"Fun dream?" he asks, a knowing smirk curling his lips.

Mortification slams into me and I jerk upright too quickly, the book sliding off my chest and thumping onto the carpet. "Oh my God."

Before he can say anything else, I bolt off the couch, abandoning both my dignity and my book, sprinting for my room while his low chuckles follow me down the hall.

"Why are you being so weird?" Levi asks me from across the kitchen island.

He'd shown up at the chalet way too early, arms full of takeout breakfast. Before I could even make up an excuse, he practically dragged me out of bed—where I'd been cocooned under the blankets, avoiding Sterling—and shoved me into the kitchen with a plate of food.

"I'm not," I mutter, the lie flat even to my own ears.

My eyes betray me as I look next to Levi and find Sterling. He's leaning against the counter, a steaming mug of coffee in his hand, and that stupid, lazy smirk tugging at his lips.

That smirk is the exact reason I'd been hiding out in the first place. It's like he's fully aware of what's going on in my head when he looks at me like that.

"You definitely are," Levi says, narrowing his eyes as he studies me. His gaze darts between me and Sterling. "Did something happen between you two?"

"What?" I blurt out, a little too loudly.

"No," Sterling answers smoothly at the same time.

The way our voices overlap makes Levi pause, brows drawing together as if he's piecing together a puzzle he doesn't want the answer to. A beat of tense silence stretches out before he finally exhales, the corner of his mouth tipping down in reluctant relief.

"Okay, good," he says at last, leaning back against the counter. "Because the last thing this world needs is another Maisy-and-Sterling shitshow."

I bristle instantly. "What does that even mean?"

"Exactly what it sounds like," Levi shoots back without missing a beat. "The last time you two messed around, it wrecked everything. Left you both in pieces, and left me feeling like I'd lost not only my sister, but also my best friend. So, forgive me if I want to make sure you're not repeating history."

Heat creeps up the back of my neck, equal parts embarrassment and anger. I stab my fork into the nearest breakfast sausage like it personally offended me, the metal scraping against the plate.

But Levi turns his attention to Sterling now, his voice firm. "Or breaking promises."

The words hang in the air and when Levi glances away, Sterling's eyes find mine. For the briefest second, I see guilt etched across his face before he looks down, jaw flexing.

I force myself to look back at Levi. "Is there a reason you're here, *brother*?" I ask, my tone a bit more aggressive than I intended.

He arches a brow at me, lowering his plate with exaggerated slowness.

"Yes, *sister*," he drawls, rolling his eyes. "I'm throwing a party here tonight."

"What?" I ask, blinking at him.

Levi lifts a finger as he chews another bite, taking his sweet time before answering. "Sterling's leaving in a week so I figured we could give him a proper send-off this time."

The room goes quiet, like someone's sucked all the oxygen out of it. My stomach knots painfully, my fork frozen halfway to my plate. Has it already been almost a month of him being here?

"You're not staying?" I ask Sterling, my voice small, betraying me.

"Why would he?" Levi answers for him, frowning like it's obvious.

Sterling chews his food slowly, watching me the whole time before finally speaking. "Well, you know how to snowboard now," he says, voice light. "And I don't exactly have a reason to stay."

Ouch.

The words reverberate in my chest like a bruise that's spreading deeper.

"Yeah, Mais," Levi adds, his tone mock-playful but lined with a hint of truth. "We've already learned that friends aren't enough of a reason for this guy to stick around."

He shoves Sterling's shoulder like it's a joke and Sterling

just rolls his eyes, brushing it off, but Levi isn't wrong. I'd been the one who said we could be friends with benefits, nothing more. So why am I surprised that he's not giving up the life he built for himself in Saltwater Springs...just to stay here with me?

"Party starts at eight," Levi says, rinsing off his plate before loading it into the dishwasher.

"Need a hand getting stuff for the party?" Sterling asks after a beat, his voice casual.

He doesn't look at me when he asks, like he's suddenly afraid of being alone with me now that Levi's reminded him of promises and past mistakes.

Levi's face brightens. "Yeah, actually. Let's go."

I watch the two of them head toward the door, leaving me behind in the kitchen with nothing but a cooling plate of food and the sour taste of regret on my tongue.

TWENTY-ONE

STERLING

THE MUSIC IS POUNDING, bass vibrating through the floors and walls. Aside from Maisy, Levi, and Courtney, I don't recognize many faces. Levi swears I know most of them from the resort or from school, but right now I feel like I've been dropped into a room full of strangers.

I shoulder my way through the crowd, brushing past a couple making out against the wall, until I reach the kitchen island where Levi's lined up bottles, mixers, and a pyramid of cheap beer cans. I crack one open and take a swig as my eyes skim the room, searching until I find her.

Maisy.

She's near the back door, surrounded by Jeff and a couple of his friends. She tosses her head back, ponytail swishing behind her as she laughs at something one of them says. Her cheeks are flushed, eyes bright with intoxication, and the way every single one of those guys is looking at her makes my stomach twist. Like they're proud she's giving them her attention.

Attention that I want.

"And here I was thinking she was your girlfriend," a voice purrs beside me.

I drag my eyes away from Maisy to find Courtney leaning against the island, bent forward, cleavage on display, lips glossed to the nines. She bats her lashes at me with a look I've seen a hundred times tonight, the same one she gave me at the skating rink. It's an invitation.

"Shouldn't you be with Levi?" I ask, my tone flat and bored.

She smirks, turning her attention lazily back to the crowd, giving a little finger wave in someone's direction. "He sent me, actually."

I follow her gaze and spot Levi across the room, beer can in his hand. He grins at me, winks, and raises his drink in a silent toast. A silent message that says 'All yours, bro.'

"Thanks," I mutter, lifting my can to my lips. "But I'm not interested."

Courtney watches me drink, a smirk tugging at her mouth, before tilting her chin toward Maisy. "I don't think she is either."

My head snaps up, finding her in the crowd again. Jeff's got his hands on Maisy now, and she's dancing against him, her body pressed close, her ass grinding into his lap while her ponytail whips side to side with the beat. My hand clenches so hard around the beer can that it crumples in my fist, liquid fizzing over my knuckles. Jeff catches my stare through the crowd, smirking like he knows exactly what he's doing, and winks.

"I'm going to fucking kill him," I growl.

"Or," Courtney purrs, her nails dragging slow, deliberate lines down my bicep, "you can just show her you can move on too."

I glance down at her, repulsion curling in my gut, but she takes my silence as permission. She slips in front of me, back pressed to the island, and her hands drift up my chest like she owns me. I look past her, back to Maisy, only to find her already watching me.

She's still against Jeff, but she's not moving now. She's frozen, eyes locked on mine as Jeff's mouth presses sloppily against her neck.

Something inside me snaps.

"Alright," I mutter, leaning forward and planting my palms against the counter on either side of Courtney's hips, caging her in. "I'll bite."

Her lips curve in triumph. "Good boy," she purrs.

The words make my skin crawl, goosebumps rising, but I let her tug at my collar as she backs us toward the dance floor. We stop in the middle of the room, bodies swaying all around us. Maisy and Jeff are directly ahead, and I see Maisy's expression shift the moment Courtney turns to face her, taking my hands and dragging them down the curves of her body until they're resting on her hips.

I let her grind against me, mechanical and detached. The whole time, I'm watching Maisy. Watching the way blood rises to her face and the way her lips part in shock and hurt.

Jeff must notice too because he slides his hands lower, gripping her waist and tugging her back into the rhythm, as if doubling down will keep her focused on him. Maisy's spine straightens and she tilts her chin high before she starts moving again, her body grinding against his as if to provoke me now. As if she's punishing me, and I take it, jaw clenching so tight it aches.

I watch as Jeff's hand slides back up, cupping her jaw, and before I even blink, he yanks her face toward his and crashes his mouth against hers. Maisy stiffens instantly, a muffled sound bursting from her throat as she shoves at his chest, breaking free with a force that sends him stumbling back a step. Her hand flies to her mouth, furious, as she wipes at her lips.

"You asshole," she spits, voice trembling with rage, and it's enough to set me off.

I shove Courtney off me and she stumbles into Levi, who curses under his breath as he steadies her. But I don't stop to check if she's okay because I have tunnel vision, blood roaring in my ears as I close the distance between me and Jeff in two strides.

He barely has time to smirk before my fist collides with his jaw. Gasps ripple through the crowd as Jeff staggers back, clutching his face, his cocky grin wiped clean off his face.

I'm on him before he can recover, fist pulled back for another blow. "Try something like that again and I'll break that ugly face of yours, dick."

Jeff spits blood, eyes flashing with anger and fear, but he doesn't move.

Smart choice.

"Sterling!" Levi shouts before his arms are around me, dragging me back before I can swing again. My chest heaves, eyes still locked on Jeff, every muscle vibrating with the need to finish what I started.

"Cool the fuck off," Levi snarls into my ear. He shoves me a step back, then turns, raising his voice above the music so that everyone can hear. "The party's over. Get out."

No one argues as people scatter instantly, muttering as they grab their coats, shoving cans into the trash on their way out. Levi doesn't let go of me until the last of the guests have disappeared into the cold, the door slamming shut behind them. Then he turns on Jeff, who's still rubbing his jaw, glaring at me from across the room.

"You're done," Levi says coldly. "Don't bother showing up tomorrow. You're fired."

Jeff's mouth falls open, but he doesn't say a word as Levi takes a warning step toward him, fists still clenched at his sides.

Without another glance in Maisy's direction, Jeff storms out, slamming the door so hard the windows rattle.

Levi exhales slowly, dragging a hand through his hair before looking at me. His eyes are furious, but under it, I see disappointment too.

"Cool off, Sterling," he says flatly. "I'll be back in the morning to help clean this shit up."

Courtney hovers near the door, her arms crossed, clearly waiting for Levi. When he stalks past, she falls into step behind him, shooting me one last wink as the door shuts behind them, leaving me and Maisy alone.

She's still standing in the open room, closer to the counter now, cheeks flushed, and arms folded tight over her chest. "You didn't have to go all caveman on him," she says, her voice trembling. "You should've just kept paying attention to Courtney. She was basically serving herself to you on a platter."

I bark out a humourless laugh, raking a hand through my curls. "That's rich, coming from the girl that was grinding her ass into Jeff like she was auditioning for a fucking 90's music video."

Her lips part, but no words come out. I don't care, though, I've waited long enough.

I step closer, my tone dropping lower. "What do you want from me, Maisy? Huh? You're the one who said you wanted to be friends with benefits. No strings attached, remember? That means I should be able to talk to whoever the fuck I want. Dance with whoever the fuck I want. Just like you." My jaw clenches. "And yet, the second you see me with another girl, it bothers you. So what do you want?"

She swallows hard, her eyes flicking to mine, brows pulled together in confusion. "I don't—"

"Don't what?" I press, closing the last bit of space between us. "Don't want me with anyone else? Don't want me touching anyone else? Then say it, Maisy. Fucking say it."

"I don't want to see you with anyone else!" she shouts, shoving me hard. "But I don't have any right to feel that way because I'm the one who ended things."

I grab her wrists, pinning them to the counter behind her as my mouth crashes into hers. The kiss is messy, angry, all teeth and desperation. She melts into it, pulling her hands free from mine and tugging at my shirt like she can't get me close enough.

I break away just long enough to growl, "You drive me insane," before lifting her straight off the floor. She gasps, legs wrapping instinctively around my waist, arms looping around my neck as I carry her toward the kitchen island.

I kiss her like I'm starving, like she's the only thing keeping me alive, tongues tangling, teeth clashing.

When my thighs hit the island, I spin, one arm tight around her while the other sweeps across the countertops, sending bottles and cans clattering to the floor. Glass shatters, liquid spilling across the tile, but I don't care. All I care about is the space I've just cleared—the space where I set her down, her ass hitting the counter hard enough to jostle a squeal out of her against my lips.

"Sterling—" she starts, but I cut her off by kissing down her throat, biting, sucking, making her whimper. My hands yank at her top, tugging it up and over her head, exposing her nipples before I cover them with my mouth.

I drag her panties down and toss them aside, leaving her skirt in place without my mouth leaving hers, and once they're off I lower her onto her back and hook her thighs over my shoulders, spreading her wide. The sight of her like this—flushed and needy, trembling under my touch—sends me into a frenzy.

"If you want me all to yourself, then I need to hear you say it," I growl before I bury my face between her legs.

My tongue drags along her pussy slowly at first, savouring how she tastes, before I dive in with the same hunger that's been clawing at me since the second she tried to push me away. Her fingers tangle in my hair, nails scraping my scalp as she moans my name, her hips bucking against my mouth.

Every sound she makes pushes me harder, deeper, until she's gasping and trembling, her thighs tightening around me. I grip her hips to hold her still, forcing her to take everything I give until she's crying out, her whole body convulsing against my tongue.

When she slows, I rise, wiping my mouth with the back of my hand before I crash my lips back onto hers, letting her taste herself on my tongue. She's still breathless, panting into the kiss, when I stand up straight and look down at her pretty pussy.

"Messy," I rasp. "That's what you do to me."

I fumble with my jeans, shoving them down just enough before I push into her in one hard thrust. Her cry is swallowed by my mouth as I grip her thighs, holding her steady while I drive into her again and again, the island creaking under her.

Her nails dig into my shoulders, her moans broken and frantic. Every slam of my hips is fueled by the jealousy of seeing her with Jeff, the frustration, and the confusion of this stupid friends with benefits situation.

I bury my face against her throat, sucking hard enough to mark her. "Say it," I growl, my voice guttural. "Say you don't want me talking to anyone else. Say you want me all to yourself."

She shakes her head, but her body tells a different story— her thighs tightening around my hips, her pussy clenching around me like she's scared to let go.

"You can't even lie to me right now," I bite out, slamming deeper, pulling a sharp gasp from her lips. "You don't want Jeff, or anyone else. You don't want anyone touching you but me. Admit it, Maisy. Admit it before I fuck the words out of you."

Her eyes flutter shut, jaw tight, refusing. I grip her chin, forcing her to look at me as I thrust harder, rougher, her body jerking with each push of my hips.

"You want more than just benefits, don't you?" My forehead presses to hers, sweat dripping down my temples. "You want *me*. All of me. No strings? That was bullshit. This—" I drive into her, deep and relentless, "—this is a string you'll never cut, baby."

"Sterling—" she gasps, her voice breaking as pleasure takes over.

I drag her closer, my hand sliding up her spine, holding her flush against me as if I can fuse us together. My lips graze her ear as I whisper, "You're mine. Not Jeff's. Not anyone's. *Mine*. Say it."

Her resolve cracks, a sob tearing free as she clings to me. "Yours. I'm yours."

The words ignite something primal in me, and I fuck her harder, my claim stamped into every thrust and bruising kiss. She chants it again, breathlessly, until neither of us can hold back any longer.

When she comes, it's with a shudder that rips through her body, her cries muffled against my shoulder. I follow, spilling into her with a groan, my grip tight on her, like I'm afraid she'll slip away if I let go.

We collapse against the island, panting and trembling. My lips brush her hair, my chest still heaving. "Don't ever try downplaying what we are again," I rasp, voice hoarse. "Because after tonight, there's no pretending this is nothing."

TWENTY-TWO

MAISY

AFTER NEARLY AN HOUR of scrubbing the countertops, tossing empty bottles and shards of broken glass away, and wiping away every trace of the party and our wild sex, Sterling threads his fingers through mine. Without a word, he leads me down the hall to the bathroom.

He shuts the door behind us and turns on the shower, letting the space grow warm. His eyes stay locked on me while his fingers trail down my body, skimming over my waist as he pushes my skirt down my hips. I shiver under the weight of his attention while he takes his time, as if stripping me down is something he doesn't want to rush.

When I'm finally standing naked in front of him, he tugs his shirt over his head with one hand and kicks his jeans free until there's nothing separating us. My heart skips a beat when my eyes land on his thick, heavy length, hard for me again.

"So beautiful," he murmurs, almost to himself, as his eyes skim over me.

His hand settles against the small of my back as he nudges

me toward the shower. I step in first, warm water rushing over my skin.

Sterling steps in right behind me, crowding me against the tile as his mouth finds my neck, lips dragging wet, open kisses down to my shoulders as his palms work my breasts greedily. By the time he turns me to face him, my chest is heaving, nipples peaked and aching, and every nerve is alive for him.

He pressed my back against the wall and nudges my thighs apart with his knee. Without needing to lift me up, his cock finds my swollen entrance, and in one relentless thrust he stretches me to my absolute limit, forcing a strangled cry from my throat. My fingers claw at his slick shoulder, searching for something to anchor me as he fills me.

"Fuck, Sterling," I gasp, head tipping back against the tile.

He growls in response, grinding deeper, his mouth claiming mine. Each thrust is harder than the last, water running down our bodies as he drives into me. It's impossibly overwhelming, but I never want him to stop.

He slows down, dragging nearly all the way out before slamming back into me, making me cry out again. The rhythm is merciless—long, teasing strokes that have me clenching tighter around him, begging without words. My thighs start to tremble as my toes barely grip the slick floor of the shower, every movement dragging me closer to the edge. Sterling reaches down, and lifts me up so that I can wrap my legs around him.

He presses his forehead to mine, eyes locking on me and stealing my breath all at once. "Feel that?" he rasps. "Feel how good I fuck you? How perfectly you take me?"

The words unravel me, tightening the coil inside until it snaps, my orgasm tearing through me in violent, pulsing waves. I cry out as I cling to him, my nails leaving half-moons on his wet skin.

He doesn't stop, though.

He keeps fucking me through it until I'm sobbing his name against his mouth, begging him to never stop.

With a broken groan, he follows me over the edge, his thrusts growing erratic before he buries himself deep and holds himself there. The shudder that rips through his body vibrates into mine, and his release spills hot inside of me.

For a long moment, the only sound is the water pattering against the tile and our ragged breathing. My body is limp against him, every muscle trembling as he kisses my temple, then my cheek, softer now, his mouth lingering like he's trying to memorize the taste of my skin.

Then suddenly, the light flickers twice before the bathroom plunges into darkness.

"Shit!" I grab onto Sterling's shoulders tightly.

"I've got you," he says, gently pulling his semi-hard cock out of my pussy and reaching past me to shut off the water.

Sterling guides us out of the shower, my bare feet touching the cool tile, and feels around until he finds his phone on the counter. He switches on his flashlight to give us some light as he glances at the screen.

"There's a blizzard warning in effect," he mutters, thumb swiping quickly. "And I have no service."

My stomach dips as I pray that Levi made it back to his house or the resort before the blizzard hit. Before I can say anything, Sterling aims his phone at the wall hooks, grabs one of the thick towels that hang there, and wraps it snugly around my shoulders before taking a towel for himself.

"Let's get your phone," he says. "Mine is about to die."

He takes my hand and leads me down the hall, the chalet eerily silent as long shadows stretch across the floor. When we reach the living room, we find my phone on an end table.

I pick it up and tap the flashlight, seeing I have fifty percent battery left. "Hopefully it's enough to last until the power turns back on."

"Keep that steady, I'll get the fire started."

The glow of my flashlight bounces weakly off the walls as Sterling stacks logs and crumpled newspaper into the fireplace and strikes a match. Within seconds, the first flames lick upward and within minutes, the faint crackle and warm orange glow fill the room.

"Better," he murmurs, before disappearing into the hall only to return with an armful of thick blankets and another towel.

I watch as he drops them onto the rug in front of the fire, before tossing the spare towel over my head with a crooked grin.

"Dry that hair before you catch a cold," he says.

I laugh, muffled by the towel as I rub it over my dripping strands. When I'm a little drier, Sterling spreads the biggest blanket out across the rug and drops down into it, tugging me with him.

I let the towel drop from my hair to the ground, the fire popping and hissing, the warmth rolling over our skin. He leans back on one elbow, watching me with complete adoration.

I wish I could just sit here, with him staring at me the way he is now, but words I haven't said yet sit heavy on my chest. I clear my throat and scooch closer to him.

"I never said thank you earlier, for what you did to Jeff." Sterling slides his hand to mine and squeezes it gently. "You didn't have to step in or hit him, but you did. For me."

His jaw tightens as he stares into the fire. "I'd do it again," he says. "And I won't apologize for it."

"I'm not asking you to," I whisper. "I'm just saying thank you." I drag the blanket tighter around my shoulders, heart pounding as I gather the courage for what comes next. "And, I need to say I'm sorry too."

Sterling blinks at me. "For what?"

My chest tightens, shame twisting in my stomach. "For the things I said to you when I ended things three years ago. I was cruel and I said things I didn't mean."

For a long beat, he just stares at me, and his silence is suffocating. Finally, he exhales. "Why won't you tell me the real reason you left me?"

"Sterling—"

He shakes his head, looking away from me. "I *loved* you. I would've done anything for you. And you cut me off like I was nothing. Like what we had was just...a mistake." His jaw clenches. "I want the truth, Maisy."

My throat tightens, tears hot behind my eyes. I force myself to look at him, because he deserves the truth I should've given him three years ago. Even if he doesn't love me anymore.

"Because I felt weak. I thought you deserved better than me," I whisper. "After the accident I wasn't myself anymore. I was so broken, so angry, and the doctors told me the road back was likely going to be long and ugly."

I swallow, digging my nails into my palm to stop the shakes. "I didn't want you chained to that—to me. I wanted you to be free to focus on your career, to chase everything you'd worked so hard for without worrying about me slowing you down."

I see shock flicker across his face, but I keep going, my voice trembling. "It wasn't because I didn't love you, or because I blamed you for what happened. God, I loved you so much it terrified me. But I thought letting you go was the only way to protect you from the mess I had become."

I swipe at my cheek, but a tear slips free anyway. "What I didn't expect was for you to give it all up. You walked away from your career. You left town." My chest aches. "That wasn't supposed to happen. That wasn't what I wanted for you."

Sterling is silent as he watches me, his jaw tight. When he finally speaks, his voice is low but shaking.

"Let me get this straight, Maisy," he says, eyes flashing angrily. "You decided what I could handle, and what I couldn't. You decided not to even give me the chance to show up for you. You chose to just shut me out. Did I understand that right?"

I open my mouth to protest, but no words come out, so I just nod because he's right. He sits forward, elbows on his knees, fingers laced together so tightly his knuckles turn white.

"Do you have any idea what that felt like? One day I'm thinking about the next competition, the next trip we could take together once you recover, the future plans we made together, and the next day I'm—" His voice cracks and he swallows hard, forcing himself to go on. "I'm standing there while the only person I've ever loved tells me it's over, that it should've never been more than friends. Like everything we were working towards didn't even matter."

I bite my lips, tears spilling faster now as he blurs before me, but I stay quiet.

He shakes his head, still staring at the fire. "I couldn't eat. I couldn't sleep. I couldn't even breathe without you. I would look at the board, at the mountains, at everything I thought I wanted, and none of it meant anything anymore. Not without you."

The blizzard rattles the windows, and a low howl blows outside the chalet. Sterling finally turns to me again. "You should've told me how you were feeling, Mais. We could've figured it out together."

"I know," I whisper. "You're right, I should've told you. I should've trusted you enough to let you in, and I'm so sorry I didn't. I've regretted it every single day."

He searches my face like he's trying to decide whether I mean what I'm saying.

I take a shaky breath, my heart pounding. "I never stopped loving you, Sterling. Not once. And being here with you now... it feels like breathing again. I tried so hard to push you away when you first got here, because I was so scared you'd realize how I actually felt. But I literally feel like I've been holding my breath for three years and I finally want to let it out."

His jaw tightens, but his eyes drop to my lips, hungry with need. Before I can second-guess myself, I lean in and kiss him. Slow at first, until he groans against my lips, one hand cupping the back of my head.

"Twice in one night wasn't enough for you?" he mumbles against my lips. "Greedy girl."

I can't stop the smile that spreads on my lips, but this time I don't let him take control. I push him back, easing him down onto the blanket, straddling his lap in front of the fire, damp hair clinging to my skin. His hands slide up my thighs and then higher as he slowly undoes my towel and tosses it to the side.

I lower my hands and unwrap his towel from his waist, adjusting myself over him so that I can push it away. I grind down against his hardening length, and his head tips back on a groan.

"Maisy," he says.

It sounds like a warning, a plea, and a prayer all in one.

"Let me," I whisper, my hands braced on his chest. "This time, let me."

His gaze locks on mine, and when I roll my hips again, he nods, jaw tight. I reach down and guide his cock to my wet entrance, sinking down slowly, inch by inch, until he's buried deep inside. My breath hitches as once again my pussy stretches around him, and he squeezes his eyes shut, a guttural curse slipping past his lips.

"I want you to feel how sorry I am...how much I love you. Every second of it."

I roll my hips, but he still bucks upwards, matching my slow rhythm, wanting me to feel every inch of him.

"You feel like home," he rasps.

Tears spill hot and fast down my cheeks again, and I cup his face between my palms, forcing him to see the truth in my eyes. "I am home," I breathe. "With you. Always with you."

His lips crash against mine, desperate, like he's been starving for me, too. I ride him slowly, dragging it out while I pour every ounce of love and regret into the way I take him.

There's no running this time. No hiding as his body tangles with mine on the rug. Every thrust feels like it's binding us back together, piece by piece. It doesn't take long for his whole body to tense, his forehead pressing against mine as a strangled groan tears from his chest. He shudders, spilling deep inside me, his release warming me from the inside out. I keep moving through it, rocking gently until his breathing evens out.

"I love you, Maisy," he finally whispers, and in this moment, I know that this is where I'm meant to be.

TWENTY-THREE

STERLING

"WOULD you ever try going pro with snowboarding again?" Maisy asks softly.

We're wrapped up in blankets in front of the crackling fireplace, the flames painting her skin gold, her head resting against my chest as she traces lazy circles on my abs with her fingertips. I feel so comfortable, so content, I'm amazed I haven't drifted off already.

I let out a low hum. "I thought about doing it for a while after I quit," I admit. "But I don't think it's my passion anymore."

She pauses her tracing for a beat and then continues, looping an infinity sign just above my navel. "What *is* your passion now?"

The answer comes easier than I expected. "Surfboards," I say, chuckling. "I love making them. There's something about customizing every detail for a surfer that feels so fulfilling, in a way snowboarding never was."

I feel her smile before I see it. "I never asked you how you got into that." She lifts her chin, her blue eyes studying me.

I shrug, a little sheepish. "Before I decided to settle down in Saltwater Springs, I traveled for a while."

Maisy's brows lift. "Where'd you go?"

I grin. "The whole world."

Her eyes widen, and she pushes up onto her elbow. "The whole world?" she repeats back to me.

"Pretty much," I say with a chuckle. "Remember that travel bucket-list you made on Pinterest? A few months before we broke up?"

Her lips part, surprised.

"I found it printed out. I don't even remember when I did it, but it was shoved between a couple of books in my room. After the accident, after you..." I trail off, swallowing hard. "When I finally packed up to leave, I found it again. And I thought, maybe if I saw the places that caught your eye, I could... I don't know, understand you better. Feel like I still had some sort of piece of you?"

Her mouth trembles, the shine building in her eyes again. She doesn't speak, but she doesn't need to.

"Anyway," I go on, my voice quieter now, "I ended up in Australia around the end of my travels, and I signed up for a few surfing lessons, just for fun. But I liked it so much that I ended up staying for a few months. I took workshops and learned the basics of shaping boards. Eventually, I found a pro shaper who agreed to take me on as an apprentice. That's where I really learned the techniques, the craftsmanship, and the traditions behind it."

"That must've been incredible," she breathes, her hand pressed flat to my chest like she can steady the beat of my heart.

I nod, smiling at the memory. "It was. Six months went by before I knew it, and when my visa ran out, I had to come back home. That's when Colton told me that his surf team was looking for a board shaper, and..." I let out a low laugh. "I don't know. It felt like fate."

Maisy is silent for a while, her gaze fixed on me, eyes shimmering. Then she lays her head back against my chest, her fingers resuming their soft, absentminded patterns over my skin.

"I'm glad you found something you're passionate about," she whispers. "That's all I ever wanted for you, Sterling. For you to have something that made you feel whole. Something that made you happy."

My hand drifts through her damp hair, fingers combing absently. "Maisy," I murmur. "You were that for me. You always were. Before snowboarding, before surfboards, before any of it—you were the thing that made me feel whole."

Her body stiffens just slightly against mine, and I feel her heartbeat quicken where her palm still rests over my chest.

I sigh, pressing a kiss to her hair. "I'm glad I found something I love doing, too. But don't think for a second it ever came close to what I felt for you. What I *still* feel for you."

For a while neither of us speaks, the fire crackling and the sound of our breathing the only noise in the room. Finally, she shifts and tilts her head back to look at me again.

"How do we even fit back into each other's lives again?" she whispers.

I let out a slow breath, running a thumb across her shoulder where the blanket slipped. "I don't know," I admit. "Saltwater Springs feels like home right now and I don't think I'm ready to leave there just yet."

Her lips part, and I see panic flash in her eyes. "But...my whole life is here. The mountain, my family—this is home. I'm not ready to leave here either." Her voice cracks and she sits up, pulling back from me.

I grab her wrist gently before she can run off again and pull her back down to my chest. "Hey," I say softly, catching her gaze. "Breathe, Maisy. We don't have to figure it all out tonight. We don't need a master plan, or answers to questions we don't even fully understand yet. We'll take it day by day."

"That's it?" A breath shudders out of her, and I squeeze her hand.

"That's it. We'll keep choosing each other, one day at a time, and we'll figure the rest out later."

I cup her face, brushing my thumb along her cheek, and pull her into a slow and gentle kiss. I don't know what tomorrow holds, but right now this is exactly where I want to be.

"I'M GOING to fucking kill him."

My eyes snap open and I feel every muscle in my body go rigid as I stare at Levi standing in the doorway, his face twisted with rage.

Maisy is still asleep, soft breaths puffing against my chest, her naked body tangled with mine under the blankets. I grit my teeth and gently shake her.

"Mais," I murmur, my eyes staying on Levi. "Wake up, Maisy."

She mumbles something against me before she blinks awake, and when she sees Levi, she screams and clutches the blanket tighter around her.

"Get out!" she shouts at Levi.

"Maisy," Levi growls, "get the fuck away from him."

I push myself up slowly, keeping one hand on the second blanket wrapped around my waist. "Levi, just listen to me. I can explain everything, but you need to calm—"

"You fucked my sister?" he roars, charging at me before I can finish.

His fist connects square with my jaw, snapping my head to the side. Pain detonates down my neck and I feel the taste of blood fill my mouth. Maisy screams, scrambling to her feet as she tightly clutches her blanket.

My hand flies up to my jaw as a throbbing heat spreads across my face. I keep my shoulders squared, the blanket clutched at my waist with one hand while the other stays lifted between us in case he tries to punch me again.

"I'm not hitting you back," I rasp through my aching jaw. "You're my best frie—"

"Oh shut the hell up, man. You promised me, as my *best friend*, that you wouldn't fuck around with my sister anymore. That you would keep the boundary while staying here with her, but instead you got in her head and got what you wanted."

"I swear to you, I didn't take advantage of her."

"I'm supposed to believe you now when you make a promise?" Levi laughs humourlessly.

"Levi, enough!" Maisy snaps, and he freezes as he looks at her. "You don't get to walk in here and treat him like that. This isn't some stupid mistake or Sterling manipulating me into putting out, okay? I wanted this."

"Maisy, you literally came up to the chalet because you didn't know what you wanted anymore." Levi scoffs before turning to look at me. "Sterling, go change and pack your shit. I'll call you a cab."

"No!" Maisy shouts, panicked, her voice cracking. "I'm going with you."

I reach for her hand, brushing my thumb across her knuckles. "Shh," I murmur softly, keeping my eyes on her even though I can still feel Levi's glare burning a fucking hole into the side of my face. "It's okay, Mais. You should

144

stay and talk to your brother after I'm gone. Maybe take some time to decide if being with me is what you really want."

Her head shakes furiously, strands tumbling across her cheeks. "No, don't do this. Don't leave me behi—"

I cup her face gently. "Hey." My voice is steady, meant just for her. "I'm not leaving you behind. But I want you to really think about us, without me being here and crowding your space and your senses. And if you still want me after you've given yourself that time, you know where to find me."

She blinks up at me, tears pooling, and I press a gentle kiss to her forehead, breathing her in like I need to memorize the moment before it's stripped away. Then I pull back, forcing my hands to drop even though it feels like tearing something out of me.

The blanket stays cinched tight around my waist as I turn and walk to the room I've been staying in. I dress in silence, then pack my things.

A gift box tumbles out of my pile of clothing, and I open it to find the ornament I never had a chance to give Maisy. I sling my bag over my shoulder, quietly place the giftbox in her room, and don't look back as I leave.

By the time I step out into the cold air, the cab headlights are already waiting at the edge of the driveway. The driver pops the trunk, and I toss my bag and board inside before sliding into the backseat.

All I can think about the whole drive is Maisy's tear-filled eyes, and the hollow weight in my chest knowing I betrayed my best friend.

Before long, Saltwater Springs greets me with its easy calm, the storm that chased me out finally gone, and the waves rolling steady against the shore.

Stepping onto the cracked pavement outside my place, I

breathe in the salt and the sense of home that settles in my chest at being back here.

I should feel whole again. I should feel like myself.

And yet I feel like there's still something missing.

Someone.

Maisy.

TWENTY-FOUR

MAISY

"HOW COULD you kick him out like that?" I shout at Levi, my voice cracking from my frustration.

My hands are shaking as I pull the blanket tighter around my naked body, as if holding onto it could somehow anchor me.

Levi runs a hand through his hair, jaw tight, and scoffs. "Maisy, how could you!? I told you how it felt for me when you two broke up—how it was like losing both of you. And you both just...you lied to my face! You both reassured me that nothing was happening, when really you two were fooling around behind my back. I gave you two the benefit of the doubt, but I should've trusted my gut."

"Levi, it wasn't like that," I say. "Sterling and I...we didn't plan this, and we didn't lie to hurt you. Yes, we weren't completely honest about what was happening when you weren't around, but it was because we were trying so hard to ignore how we felt. Sterling tried so hard to push me away."

"Yeah, it sure looked that way when I walked in on you two butt ass naked on the fucking floor," he scoffs. "I rushed over here because both of your phones went straight to voicemail and I wanted to make sure the blizzard hadn't, oh I don't know, *killed* you both. But I honestly wish I'd just stayed away."

I internally curse my phone for dying in the middle of the night. I could've prevented Levi from walking in on us like this if it'd just had enough charge to take his call.

"I know it seems like he and I betrayed you—"

"Because you did," he interrupts, but I keep going.

"But, like I said, we tried so hard to fight it. It just got to this point where we realized that it wasn't fair to keep doing that—to him, or to me. I can't pretend anymore that I don't care. I love him. I never stopped loving him. And I never should've let him go."

His fists clench at his sides, but I see the hurt in his eyes from being kept in the dark, along with fear for me. I realize that he's just being my protective older brother who just wants to keep me safe.

"I know I broke your trust," I whisper. "And I'm sorry. I wish I could've handled this better."

Levi exhales, jaw tightening as he studies me. I hold his gaze, willing him to see that I'm telling the truth—that this isn't reckless. He finally exhales, running a hand over his face, shaking his head.

"Hurry up and get dressed," he mutters.

I blink at him, confused. "Where are we rushing off to?"

He rolls his eyes. "You have a boyfriend to chase, don't you?" He smirks.

I give him a small smile but shake my head. "No, Sterling is right. We need some time apart. If we rush back into this with any sliver of doubt, it's not going to work."

Levi studies me for a long beat, his hands sinking into his pockets. Finally, he nods once. "Alright," he says, already moving toward the door. "But when you're ready to go after him, call me first. I want to make him sweat a little."

I roll my eyes, tugging the blanket tighter around me. "You're impossible."

He laughs as he shuts the door behind him, the chalet falling quiet around me. For a moment I just stand there, breathing in the silence, letting the ache settle in my chest. Then I drift back toward my room, every step heavy.

When I push the door open, I stop short. A small velvet box waits on the centre of my bed. My lips part, hands trembling, as I pick it up. I lift the lid and find the glass ornament from the Winter Festival—two skis crossed together, catching the light. The gift is so Sterling that it makes me laugh through the tears burning my eyes.

I press the box to my chest, letting the sob come anyway. But this time, beneath the ache, there's a knowing. He still loves me. And I know that I love him enough to chase him down. I don't need to wait. I race to plug my dead phone into the charger, changing while I desperately wait for it to turn on so that I can call Levi to come back.

When the screen lights up, I call him right away.

"Maisy, is everything okay?"

"Get back here," I say breathlessly. "I need help packing."

"What?" he asks, confused. "Where the hell are you going now?"

"I'm moving." I stand up straighter now and smile. "To Saltwater Springs."

"Jesus fucking ch—" He stops short, taking a deep breath. "Alright, I'll be there in ten minutes."

TWENTY-FIVE

STERLING

I PUSH open the shop door, my boots scuffing the worn floorboards as the familiar scent of old wax, salt, and sawdust washes over me like a long-lost friend. The place feels smaller somehow, as if time itself tightened the walls while I was gone, but the racks are just as I left them—a crooked army of boards leaning against the walls, each one a different curve. My fingers trail along their rails as I pass, and I can't hold back my grin.

I haul my duffel up the narrow stairs to my attic apartment, and drop my bag on the floor, strip off my jacket, and for a moment I just stand in the doorway, letting the quiet settle in. Sunlight beams in through the blinds as I run a hand through my curls and feel a steady hum of being exactly where I belong. For once, it feels good to come back to a place I'm starting to think of as home.

A few hours later, once I've unpacked and tossed in a quick load of laundry, I take the steps back down two at a time only to find Gabriel, coach of the Saltwater Shredders, standing in the middle of my shop. He's the kind of man who manages to look like he just stepped off a surf break and into a boardroom—flawless and powerful.

"Welcome back from Hawaii," I say, walking up to him with my hand outstretched.

He looks up from the board he was examining, and flashes me a grin as he puts it back and shakes my hand. "Thanks. We got back two days ago. And—" he lets go and claps his hands together, "I have a job for you."

"A job?"

He nods. "We're creating an official beta team. Saltwater Shredders 2.0. We want a roster of boards custom-shaped to each surfer. This'll be detailed work, at least a two-year commitment, full-time shaping and collaborating with the riders. Are you in?"

Two years.

Every part of me wants to scream yes. It's a dream opportunity, one that excites me straight to my core. But right before I give him an answer, I remember that it's not just me anymore. Me and Maisy are a team now, and I need to know that she'd be okay with the fact that I'd be here for at least another two years, if not longer.

"Can I think on it?"

Gabriel studies me like he's weighing the man I was against the man I've become over the last month.

"Let me guess," he says, voice threaded with amusement. "You met someone back in Bluewater Bluffs?"

I laugh and rub the back of my neck. "Something like that."

At that exact moment the front door swings open and my whole world shifts on its axis as Maisy steps in, reducing everything to a single, searing focus: her.

"You're here," I say in disbelief, standing up straighter now.

She nods, a huge grin spreading on her face. "I'm here."

She closes the distance between us in two long strides and

the room collapses into the soft, slow orbit we always fall into. I pull her into me, and she fits against my chest like a missing piece.

"I thought you were going to take some time to make sure this is what you want," I mumble into her hair.

She laughs against me. "I don't need time, Sterling. This *is* what I want."

Gabriel clears his throat with a courteous cough, breaking the moment.

"I'm Gabriel, coach for the Shredders." He holds out a hand and Maisy shakes it without missing a beat. "I actually saw you in the last Olympics. Impressive stuff. Shame to hear that you quit after the accident."

She flushes, awkward and deflecting. "It wasn't—I don't think I could've kept up that pace after the accident."

Gabriel's grin is soft. "Let me know if you ever want to give surfing a try. You've got the frame of a competitor."

He winks at her, and then he turns back to me. "Think about the job. I want you, Sterling. We'll need your answer soon."

When the door shuts behind him and the shop settles, Maisy turns to look at me curiously. "He asked me to take on a huge job with a secondary team he's putting together."

"Sterling, that's amazing! You have to say yes. It's what you love doing." I force a small smile, and she frowns as she studies me. "What's wrong?"

"It's a two-year commitment. I just want to be sure you're okay doing this long-distance thing for that long of a time."

She laughs quietly, as she presses her hands to my chest, eyes bright. "Well, I guess that just means we'll be in Saltwater Springs for the next two years."

"We?" I echo.

She nods as her lips tug up on one side. "I'm moving here.

I'll always be able to drive back to Bluewater Bluffs whenever I miss home. I can always visit my family. But I want to try this new life. Here. With you."

I sweep her up without thinking, spin her in a circle, and kiss her, pouring all of my love into it. She laughs against my mouth, breathless, and then rests her forehead to mine, hands tucked into the back of my shirt as she strokes my neck.

The shop bell jingles and Levi steps in holding a large suitcase, shoulders squared, expression unreadable for a beat, the air between us taut. I lower Maisy back down and stare at him as he walks up to me like he means business. He stops a breath away sliding the suitcase toward me, and I hold my ground because if he punches me again, I'll swing back this time.

"Take care of my sister," he says, surprising me.

"I will," I reply.

He nods and turns to leave. "Wait," I call out as he reaches the door.

He slowly turns to look at me, and I don't miss the way his jaw tightens.

"Levi, I'm sorry." I untangle myself from Maisy and walk up to him at the door. "I should've told you how I was feeling."

"Why didn't you?" He buries his fists in his pockets, probably to stop himself from hitting me again.

I force out a chuckle. "Honestly? Because I thought if I told you, I'd lose you. And if I lost you, then I'd lose Maisy too. I didn't think I was allowed to want her, not after the accident, not after the promise I made."

"You don't get it. I didn't need you to have it all figured out. I just needed you to tell me the truth. Do you know what it felt like finding out this way? Like I never even knew you at all."

"I know." My throat works around the words. "And I hate that I made you feel that way. You're right, I should've trusted you. I was scared, but that's no excuse. I'll never lie to you again."

Levi studies me for a long while before he speaks again. "Good," he mutters finally. "Because if you do, we're done. For good."

I nod. "I understand."

He huffs out a breath, like he's trying to release the weight of it all. Then, with a small shake of his head, he adds, "You're an idiot, Sterling. But you're her idiot now. Don't screw it up."

A smile tugs at the corner of my mouth. "I won't."

Maisy returns to my side, squeezing my hand. For a wild second I imagine all the small, ordinary mornings ahead: coffee that gets cold because our hands are tangled, sand tracked through the workshop, nights where we fall asleep to the sound of the ocean. I think of Gabriel's offer—the steady, permanent work that I'm actually looking forward to, the people I'll build boards for, the craft I love.

Two years suddenly feels like it could be a new beginning.

Maisy squeezes my hand, eyes soft as they lock on mine, and my chest swells, full of everything I can't seem to put into words.

"How'd I get so lucky to get you back?" I ask, leaning in and kissing the side of her head.

Her lips curve into a smile as she looks up at me. "Blame the blizzard."

I huff out a laugh, and smirk at her.

"Gross," Levi says, his lips pulled back in disgust. "Get a room."

Maisy and I burst out in laughter, and I throw my hand over Levi's shoulder as I start walking us out of the shop. "Come on, let me show you around town."

ACKNOWLEDGMENTS

Writing a book may look like a solo sport, but it truly takes a team. I'm lucky to have the best one.

To my best friend and beta reader, Chelsea — thank you for always being my sounding board, my hype woman, and the person who tells me when I'm being dramatic (and when the drama should stay in the book).

To my family — thank you for stepping in to wrangle the kiddos so I could disappear into snowy mountains and fictional chaos. Your support means more than you know.

To my husband — this story exists because of you. One long road trip, one concert, and one offhand idea later... and suddenly we had a whole new world of love, snowboarding, and second chances. Thank you for believing in Sterling before I even knew who he'd become.

To Arifa, for the mountain adventure that sparked scenes in these pages and for being by my side through every plot twist —real or imagined.

To Ramona, my editor — thank you for your sharp eyes, precision, and incredible speed. You helped shape this story into its best form.

To Books and Moods, for always turning my messy inspiration into covers that feel like magic.

And to my ARC readers — thank you for being as excited about Sterling and Maisy as I was. Your early enthusiasm keeps me going every time.

This book holds a little piece of me. Maisy's determination to stay strong, even when she's breaking a bit on the inside, is a reflection of my own journey toward letting myself be vulnerable — both on the page and off. I wrote her to remind myself that love doesn't require perfection, just courage.

Finally, to you, dear reader: thank you for taking a chance on my first-ever novella (*so* close to a novel — we were right there!). You're the reason this journey is worth every late night, and every rewrite. I hope this story reminds you that second chances are real, love is worth fighting for, and sometimes coming home is the bravest thing we can do.

Thanks for reading and for making this dream such a fun ride!

ABOUT THE AUTHOR

Tanisha Headley is a Canadian romance author whose stories —whether light or dark—always centre broken characters learning to feel whole again. Whether she's writing small town slow burns or twisted, emotional rollercoasters, her books explore healing, identity, and the kind of love that wrecks and rebuilds you.

When she's not crafting characters who feel too real to be fictional, Tanisha is drinking too much tea, listening to moody playlists, or daydreaming about the next story that won't leave her alone. More often than not, though, she's climbing mountains (literally), dancing in the kitchen, or making memories with her husband and kids—the best parts of her real-life love story.

instagram.com/authortanishaheadley